Muscle Studs

Arian Mabe

This is a collection of short stories featuring anthropomorphic characters and is intended for adult audiences only.

This book covers the following content and kinks: gay furry sex, oral sex, anal sex, risky public and semi-public sex, group sex, light to moderate domination/submission play and an appreciation of fit, anthropomorphic bodies!

Table of Contents

In the Showers

Sean grunted, the stallion hefting the weight up over his head, shoulders trembling. He could just about feel the bar bending above him, the barbell loaded with so much iron that others in the gym were giving him looks, his bay hide pouring with sweat. Yet he didn't care for how he looked in the middle of a lift, groaning, drawing attention to himself without even thinking about it, legs braced.

Up and up – not using any other muscles, not cheating. It had to go up and the horse practically snarled as he forced his body through the lift through sheer force of will, pressing up into an overhead press and pausing there, shaking. There was no "gently down" of the weight when it came but he tried to break its drop to the safety pins the best he could, huffing and heaving, ears twitching, sweeping his forelock back from his muzzle as the rack juddered, the pins holding fast. It was a good thing they were there sometimes when he just couldn't get it back onto the barbell hook from where he'd started, although it would be more difficult still to re-set for his next exercise.

That didn't matter though, not all that much, as long as he got what he wanted from his workout and the stud of a stallion threw his head back as he took a deep glug of water from his bottle, droplets trickling down around his lips and muzzle. Someone whistled from elsewhere in the gym but he could not pay them the attention they wanted over the burn of his muscles, aching for another set but knowing that it was not the day to push his body past the limits that had already been tested. It would only slow him down.

Sean didn't look like a stallion that could lift that much despite being powerfully built but building efficient muscle was his game and he had no inclination to gain mass alone. What was the point of muscle if it was only for show? Of course, he liked the look of it too on other guys but he was all about functionality, driving himself on harder and harder as the season progressed, aiming for lifting competitions that would see him set right at the very top of his category. When he trained for strength alone, it didn't matter too if he had a tiny bit of a muscle-gut, abs strong but hidden as he groaned and bent over to pick up his towel and chalk from the Olympic matting.

He knew there were eyes on him and, workout complete, he played it up, flicking his tail and flagging it, showing off just how he knew his loose, comfortable workout sweats hung over the muscle of his ass. Not that he was going to let anyone get up under his tail but he wouldn't mind taking a nice, tight hole too if he had the chance that day. And, at his gym, filled with grunting, sweating, eager bodies, there was *always* that chance.

"Hey, hon."

Sean smirked, winking at the mare that passed him, striding past as if to stomp, her mind focused on her workout to come. She'd surely have eyes on her too in the gym, though he preferred those of the male persuasion when it came to after-hours pleasures, lust running strife through a setting that was practically designed to raise lusts and the snarl of testosterone.

She'd have her fun too but, well...it was time for him to go cool off a shade.

And he could not have found a better partner in the showers, the small otter half-turning as he entered, showering facing the wall. It was a communal shower room there but that wasn't something that bothered Sean as he grunted in the back of his throat, admiring the lithe form of the otter. He had more of a swimmer's body with not an ounce of spare fat on him, ribcage showing lightly through his wet, slicked-down fur, but he didn't need to build fat and muscle to draw Sean's attention, simply a willing player in the expenditure of lust that had to be taken advantage of.

"Er..."

The otter glanced back again but he didn't move away even as Sean stalked inside, a towel around his waist only to be hung up outside the communal shower entrance. With that, he revealed the thickness of his sheath, already plumping out with the swell of his cock, his fat, stallion-orbs churning below, ready with need and a load of cum that he had not unloaded in a week. Licking his lips, the stallion chuffed softly, nostrils fluttering, offering it to the otter with a sweep of his paw.

"Well, what are you waiting for?"

The otter, whose name he didn't know, hesitated, another non-committal sound teetering on his lips, but there was only one thing that he could do. No male there had managed to resist Sean yet and the stallion's broad chest puffed up as, tentatively, the otter stepped out from under his shower nozzle, the stream of water splattering on the rough tiles behind him.

"There's a good, boy," Sean nickered, pleased at the already had someone suitable to help him work off some need. "I'm sure someone like you knows just what to do with this."

He groped his nuts, fingers running up to his sheath, stroking it, helping his cock out into the open air, though it would soon be gulped down by another with a much better muzzle for it. That was alright though as the otter licked his lips, putting one hind paw in front of the other, so very slowly closing the distance between them as if hypnotised, his eyes fixed to that throbbing length of growing horse-meat.

There was plenty more of it to come too even as the otter dropped to his knees, knocking them on the hard floor and not caring for the bruises that he would later find. All that mattered for him right there and then was that cock before him, questing for his lips, the tip soft and flat, the slit drooling with pre-cum already. The stallion was lustful, so very much so, towering over him, muscles everywhere, a stud of a creature that he would be honoured to worship.

Sean's fingers pressed behind his head, drawing him in, grinding his muzzle up along the length of his cock, rubbing down over that smooth, dark shaft and teasing the medial ring. It was all the otter needed to get started and Sean groaned, tail flagging proudly, as the otter kissed along his shaft, luxuriating in the softly sweet sensation. Although his shoulders ached, he trusted the otter to do his best work and stretched his arms up over his head, working out the strains and kinks of his workout, glutes clenching, a nicker of need already tickling at the back of his throat.

Others looked in but didn't stay, knowing that Sean was one who rather preferred his muscle-sluts to come one at a time, even though it was his orgasm that was of the greatest importance, of course. He snorted and huffed, nostrils quivering, stomping a huge hoof into the ground, fetlocks defined without a trace of feather like some of the heavier breeds of horses. He was beautiful in his own, masculine way and nobody would ever contest that as the otter whimpered and tried to get his cock into his mouth, straining his mouth wider and wider. Sean chuckled.

"Let me help you with that..."

It was help but help that benefitted him more than the otter as the smaller fur squirmed and wriggled, tail thwapping the floor. It was hard for him to take such a large cock but Sean wasn't about to take "no" for an answer when it was so very clearly something they both wanted, hooking a thick finger into the corner of the otter's mouth to make him open up even wider. Although the stallion's thick length was devastatingly meaty, he was forced to take it, swallowing rapidly, inch after inch of that huge cock fed into his mouth and the back of his throat.

"Take it down..."

Sean coaxed him along even as the fatness of his cock pushed the otter beyond all limits he'd thought he had, bearing through. He had to take it though, inches teasing into his throat, the otter struggling to breathe – but that was something that Sean could allow when he was ready for the otter to gulp a breath down. He didn't have to worry about such trivial, little things anymore when he had a dominant stud to consider that for him, to take care of him.

Well, that was if he took care of Sean's throbbing hard-on first, pleasing that stud-cock as it so very dreadfully deserved to be pleased. It was a crime to leave such a fat cock without the attention that it deserved and the otter moaned around him, though the sound came out so muffled that he may as well have not bothered at all. That was alright though, for Sean could still take his pleasure from him, rocking his hips and using the force of his lower body to drive in, fingers running over the top of the otter's head, the slightly thicker hair there giving him something to grip around his ears.

"Yesss..."

Sean grunted, ears flicking back and forth, though all he could hear was the lewd slop of his cock disappearing into the otter's throat as he thrust and thrust, trusting that throat to take him down. The showers were still running and the rushing hiss proved a soothing backdrop to a release that he so very badly needed, moaning out loud, not caring one bit who heard him. That moment was all for him, only for him, the otter just a willing participant in the release that Sean would have had either way if he had not been there. If not for the otter, he would have found someone else, the otter simply in the right place at the right time. That had been known to happen before and he wasn't the sort of stallion to complain.

He always got what he wanted anyway.

Sean rolled his shoulders back, hips thrusting, working out his cool-down in the best way possible. He had so much to give and drove his cock deep into that needy throat, the otter snatching breath between thrusts, tiny chest shuddering as he coaxed it from him. Drop after thick drop of pre-cum flowed from him as if he was actually in the middle of climaxing, yet the stallion was no weaker male, a beta male, one who could only get off once and then be done with it. Already, the need to climax rose within him but once would never be enough for a stud like him as he thrust with unbridled abandon, bucking his hips like a wild stallion reminiscent of his ancestors.

The otter was just there to take it, nothing more than a hole for him to fill, though he would have his enjoyment from it too. Even then, the otter's cock was out, a firm rod of considerably smaller flesh, the difference between their girths almost laughable, though it was just how the otter was. Maybe he was a size queen and that was quite alright too, everyone having their different needs and inclinations, though all Sean needed was a tight, willing hole to fuck, whether it was a tail hole or a mouth, a yawning gape that drew him in more and more.

The otter was just the ticket, just what he needed, his tongue pressing up to the underside of his cock as the stallion stomped, the dull echo ringing through the shower room. There was no need for him to hold back as he whinnied out his triumph, announcing to everyone just what he was getting up to, not that anyone at that gym would be surprised. It was practically a tradition, by that time, for Sean to get his rocks off after working out. It was a rare occasion indeed that he didn't get the sweetly musky treat of emptying his load down the throat or under the tail of a willing slut and the otter did not disappoint, whimpering and swallowing repeatedly, taking down every last drop of that thick treat that he was so kindly offered.

All he could do was swallow and swallow, his chest and throat tightening, the bulge of that cock obviously showing through his throat. Sean was too wrapped up in his pleasure to care, grunting and groaning, a spatter of water flowing over his head as their movement set off another of the motion sensitive nozzles, soaking his mane flat to his neck, forelock streaming down his face. It streamed down his muscles in rivulets, highlighting their definition as ropes of thick, creamy stallion-seed poured straight down the otter's throat without even a chance for him to taste it. Not a drop was wasted.

"Unff... Good... To start."

Coughing and licking his lips, chest heaving for lost breath, the otter knelt there, blinking dumbly up at the stud horse, who had his still-hard cock in one paw, jacking it off slowly. It had tried to soften but it took hardly any stimulation at all for him to stay hard, the shower washing off the otter's saliva – not that it would have done him any good anyway. He was in it for the long haul as the stud horse pushed him lightly, more guiding him than anything else, onto all fours, the otter's tail already invitingly raised. Even if his mind was struggling to catch up with all that was going on, acting the part of a side-character when he was in the leading role, he was ready for it, the pucker under his tail relaxing at just the right moment.

It took nothing at all for Sean to push in, drawing the otter's hips back to his as he penetrated him. It all happened as if in a dream with the deliriously hot water washing over the two of them, more voices drifting in from the locker rooms. But they didn't care about that as he slowly, inch by tantalising inch, fed every last bit of that monstrous cock deeply up into the otter's tail hole.

There was no lube but that was no matter to either of them as long as they went slowly, the otter's forbidden entrance opening up around him as if in offering. It was a gift that Sean gladly took as he snorted, hips rocking, thrusting lightly, checking what the otter was ready for. Despite his innate dominance, knowing what he wanted and taking it, he had no intention of hurting the otter either, pre-cum spilling out to at least lubricate the path of his cock a tiny bit. He didn't need that lubrication but it was comforting to know it was there for the otter, grinding in deep, rocking his hips, working up to the body-shaking thrusts that the stud-horse loved so much.

"Fuck... That's the stuff..."

Sean groaned deep in the back of his throat, head rolling back, though he didn't have to worry about how he was perceived. He was the stud in charge and that was all that he needed to be, powering in, the force of his thrusts growing and growing. Not an inch of his cock was spared as he slopped in past the medial ring, throbbing and pulsing, the otter's anal ring squeezing around him. If he was trying to drag him deeper though, there was not a single inch of his cock left, the thick length ploughing him full as he was pleasurably forced, with a squeal, to spend his otter-load over the floor.

Yet it was nothing in comparison to the load that the otter had taken down his throat only moments before, his own pleasure washed away in the showers as voices clamoured in, interest peaked.

"Look at that slut..."

"Damn, he can really take it..."

"Yeah, he's Sean's bitch now."

"Lucky whore!"

The envy in their voices was palatable and the otter flushed with an odd sense of pride as he was filled, bearing back against Sean's thrusts with all the strength left in his body, as little as that had been. But that was all he could do as the stallion ramped up, using and abusing him in the best way possible, fur soaked and slicked down to their bodies as they took their pleasure in carnal fashion.

Sean neighed proudly, tail flagging, heralding his orgasm as he exploded once again, his huge nuts jiggling as he ploughed the otter's tight hole full. Ropes of thick, virile seed planted themselves right where they belonged as other curious patrons of the gym watched on, whistling at just how the stallion's glutes tensed, pounding the otter even through his climax. It was his driving, almost violent thrusts that forced his cum back out down the length of his cock, drooling and splattering, though there was always more to cum. A stallion's orgasm was legendary and there were many reasons that other furs were jealous of them, Sean's nostrils flaring as he clenched his teeth and drew the otter as far back onto his shaft, brushing his sheath in an intimate kiss, as possible.

"Yes... Fuck..."

But he didn't need to say any more than that as the otter's head hung, sexually sated and trembling. Hell, he'd been satisfied with the first load down his throat and anything else over that was a bonus, tail wagging faintly, though he was not of the canine persuasion. It was hard to show his appreciation from such a position but he did his best as the stud's cock finally softened just a little, his tail hole relaxing its grip, for his body could not contain such pressure for so long.

Sean smirked, pulling out, the otter's hole left gaping in a messy cream-pie of cum, though that was just a little reminder of what had come to pass there. The stud would return for his regular session the next evening and he would find a submissive little slut of an otter waiting for him in the showers, on his knees with his mouth obediently open already.

He grinned. That was how they all were, dropping to their knees for him, one after the other, worshipping his cock and his muscles.

A fresh towel – not the one he had brought – was waiting for him outside the showers and he flicked one ear towards the gathered furs, a mix of shapes and sizes.

"Something you like?"

He didn't wait for an answer, strutting off with his head held high, tail flagged and a cheeky little swing in his hips. He knew what they liked. He knew what he liked. What more did he have to worry about?

There'd always be sluts at a gym for a stud to have their way with... That was one thing he was sure of. And he'd always be there also to feed their whorish needs.

There was nowhere else he'd rather be.

Sauna Slut

Jonty rested his elbows on his thighs as he inhaled the softly scented steam in his most frequented room at the gym complex. Not many steam rooms attached to fitness facilities were infused with relaxing aromas, unless they were the "frou-frou" kind he would not want to be seen at anyway, yet the equine found the scent pleasing, unknotting sore muscles and clearing his sinuses.

No, facilities were all well and good, but his kind of gym posed a far more pleasing clientele. Gym bunnies did not fall easy on his eyes and he could not understand the appeal towards losing weight, obsessing over pounds when the sheer goal was to be skinny. Or the mindset of those that went to health clubs simply to sweat it out in the sauna. Did they not know that it would not make them lose any true weight at all?

His nostrils flared, breathing in lavender. It relaxed his mind and aching body, pummelled into nothing but a quivering mass of abused horse beneath the weights of his session. No, health club gyms and spas were a pleasant enough visit from time to time, but they were not Jonty's style. He wanted a gym with *real* males, the ones that sweated out their anger and frustration after a long day of work and idiotic bosses that clucked in their ears, driving them out to escapes beyond ordinary reach. The horse's grey lips twitched into a wry smile. Luckily, this particular gym outstripped his expectations in terms of equipment, space, facilities and, of course, clientele.

Brushing his mane off the arch of his gleaming, brown neck, black strands sticky with sweat in the moist heat, and flicked a loose black strand off his hoofed fingertips. Stupid thing – always getting in the way. Sometimes he envied the mares with their mane-clips and hair ties that tamed the unruly beast of a mane, at least for a time, but that would be a little too gay for his liking. Not that he had anything against guys, of course. That would be ironic, if it had been true. Gay males were the main reason that he attended the gym at all. That and lifting. Sometimes.

He licked sweat from his lips, shifting to hide the bulge in his "sauna shorts." They were exactly the same as swim shorts or swim trunks, only something he took to the gym for the sauna and steam room and showers only, preferring to keep the dark blue pair for the tension easing portion of his day. There was something soothing about slipping into them. The only problem he had with the gym was that there was no pool attached. Jonty rolled his head back, working out a crick in his neck. Males in tight swimwear were also a very good thing, very good indeed.

Shaking his head, the horse's forelock fell away from his face to expose a white, heart-shaped marking in the centre of his forehead. Although it was clearly a heart, something friends and strangers liked to point out on a daily basis, in equine marking terms, it was a "star." Bloody star. Everyone mentioned it – and he really did mean *everyone*.

The horse huffed, eyes hazing over as his head swam with heat. A tremor ran up his leg and a muscle twitched, convulsing against his will. It had been too long.

Pushing himself to his hooves with a groan, soreness already setting in from his workout, Jonty stretched his arms out above his head with a crackle of joints popping. Not for the first time, he wished the gym had a Jacuzzi handy. There was nothing like a soak in a hot tub after deadlifting. He smiled, admiring the muscle in his legs through the steam, even as he swayed drunkenly from side to side, muscles flexing proudly. His progress truly was showing.

Ducking quickly out of the steam room, the horse shuddered at the rush of cool air, tail flicking over his haunches. He grumbled as he stepped into the open shower, inhaling sharply at the sudden blast of cold water right in the muzzle, streaming over his cheekbones.

His mane soaked down flat to his neck as he rinsed off the sweat, hooves shining with trickling droplets of water. Jonty shuddered, lips flapping as he bore the cold, a rarely desired shock to the system. Whinnying, he turned in a circle to clear the sweat from his back as swiftly as possible, spinning too quickly to thoroughly clean himself. The horse's teeth chattered.

"Fucking *hell*," he muttered, hopping from hoof to hoof with a clack-clack-clack on the tiles. "Fuck, fuck, fuck, come on..."

Behind him, someone giggled, and he glared over his shoulder at the suspect chestnut mare, arms crossed primly across the front of her bikini top. A familiar face at the gym, he had chatted to her some, many months ago, before being dragged out to dinner and get togethers – all against his will if he was questioned on the matter. Her sense of humour was not for all, it had to be said, though he liked her well enough, that cheeky red mare. Smoothing over his expression, Jonty straightened and cleared his throat, still shivering beneath the deluge.

"What?"

Stomping from the shower, he lunged for his towel to rub the water from his face and forelock, scrubbing until his skin rang raw beneath his short brown coat. She laughed again, making no attempt to hide her mirth as her eyes crinkled in at the corners.

"Nothing, just never heard a stallion squeal like a filly before. Well...not without doing certain things to said stallion first, of course. They usually take some persuasion to whinny quite like that."

Jonty's ears flipped flat to his skull and he scowled, expression twisting darkly.

"Oh, screw you, mare," he snapped. "Why've you always got to have some snappy comment? Can't a bloke fucking shower in peace?"

She frowned, amusement vanishing in the face of her friend's short temper. He skirted her, swiping a swift, gulping drink from the water fountain before making as if to stalk back to the changing rooms with no further words said, tail swishing furiously. What was her problem? His problem, if it could be said to be such a thing, softened and retreated into its sheath, though his groin still ached with a familiar need.

Damn this!

"Hey now, don't be like that." She stepped into his path and held her paws up – or "hands," depending on how a horse anthro thought of them, there was really no big difference there. "What's got you so worked up today? Didn't you have a good night with Deon after all that then?"

Jonty balked and she stepped closer, pressing.

"Come on. What's up with you?"

Jonty shook his head and shrugged, sliding his gaze away.

"What would make you think that? What about Deon?"

He tried to slip away, but the mare was insistent, raising an eyebrow and gently blocking his path.

"Your general attitude of seriously needing to get some right now?"

"Get some?"

He rolled his eyes. The mare smirked.

"To get *fucked*, pony. You know I'd help out with that if you swung my way. I have toys, you know."

He snorted, the horse's eyes softening at the corners where they had tightened into hard, humourless lines.

"Thanks, sweetheart, but I think I'll pass this time. You get to choose the size of your dicks."

"That I do!" She chirped, wrapping a towel around her torso as a couple of canines emerged from the adjacent sauna, both shaking sweat from their fur. "If it helps any, there's a few fit guys hanging in the sauna, new ones. May tickle your fancy there, hon, if you know what I mean..."

Jonty rolled his eyes for a second time, an action that was becoming quite common around the mare. Predictable, as always. Predictable, predictable, predictable.

Yet not unwelcome.

"Oh...shut up..."

Jonty's attention wavered, hooves edging towards the sauna almost without conscious thought. Knowing that she had hit home, she grinned and blew him a kiss, fluttering her fingers in mock farewell.

"Don't say I never did anything for you now. See you next Tuesday!"

Shrugging, he deigned to wave his paw in goodbye as the mare disappeared around the corner, a grey and white furred husky with wandering eyes licking his lips as she passed. Jonty's stomach plummeted in momentary disappointment: he had had his eye on that husky for a while, watching how the curve of muscle showed through his fur more and more with every passing week. He'd been as skinny as a stick when he had joined the gym and it was no secret amongst Jonty's circle of friends he'd wanted some private time with the husky for a good while now. Dedication to the progression of one's ability was a sexy trait indeed in Jonty's eyes.

It was a shame that the black and white husky looked to be straight after all. All the best ones were. Jonty smirked, rubbing the back of his paw across his muzzle. Though the straight lads could be turned the other way, with the right sense of...persuasion.

Grinning, Jonty wrapped his towel around his waist – unneeded modesty – and peered into the sauna, ears twitching. Though the interior was dark, he could just about discern the shapes of various legs in the dim, soft lighting, muscled calves and boulder thighs enticing him inside.

No harm in meeting new furs... He reasoned with himself as he opened the door, stepping inside to a rush of dry heat. *Then again...who knows what might happen? Much, if I know myself at all by now.*

The horse bit the inside of his cheek, swallowing his smile as he stepped into the sauna, pausing in the entrance. As his eyes adjusted to the light, he picked out the shapes of four others sitting on the three tiers, position dependant on the level of heat they desired. Higher tiers equalled greater heat and it was not advised to stay at the top for any great length of time; warnings plastered the walls in heat and moisture resistant plastic.

Seating himself, he took a closer look at his fellows, starting with the creature closest to him. Another hoofed anthro sat a couple of feet away, stripes immediately classifying him as a zebra. On the middle tier sat a wolf and a lion, murmuring to each other in low voices as the grey wolf's tail wagged gently between his legs, hanging down against the wooden bench. Last but certainly not least was the crocodile at the very top, jaws parted to release heat from within his body, leathery skin perfectly suited to the environment of the sauna. If he had been alone, Jonty would have let out a long, low whistle.

Damn, that mare has good taste.

As different as their species were, their physiques demonstrated their prowess, muscles bulging for sheer purpose rather than self-admiration. He would not put it past them to all engage in some manner of physical sport. Perhaps it was wrestling? He could not say he was familiar with the intricacies of the body required, he was sad to say.

Conversation between strangers was not unusual in the sauna but Jonty contented himself with listening to the burble of talk behind him and sneaking sidelong glances, tail flicking lazily against the wooden bench.

The lion rubbed his fingers through his thick mane, teeth showing as he panted with an open-mouth and laughed at a joke the zebra made that Jonty was not quite close enough to overhear. The zebra, being the closest, garnered the most attention and Jonty watched, mesmerised, as his dark nostrils flared with each inhalation, a drop of moisture cradled in the teardrop hook of the one nostril, struggling with the heat as much as he enjoyed it. He would have done better in the sun with white stripes to reflect the rays, Jonty considered.

Like the pendulum of a clock, his thick, ropey tail swayed, drawing the horse's attention down his shaped, muscled legs. Even his calf was defined – a tough aesthetic for any equine to achieve and one that only showed itself through years of hard work.

Jonty's heart jumped as the zebra looked directly at him, brown eyes piercing in their intensity. He raised an eyebrow at the curious horse and smirked, lips quirking up to show a flash of pink tongue, startling in the black and white landscape of his body. Though Jonty immediately looked away, he knew that he had been seen and he felt the zebra's eyes boring into him in turn, taking in every inch. But was his gaze judgmental or falling into simple admiration? He could only hope. There was no way to tell without making eye contact again and Jonty's natural shyness tied his tongue into an inescapable knot.

Blushing, though the heated colour could not be seen through his short coat, Jonty looked down at his hooves, cursing himself for being too obvious, yet again. It was his fucking downfall, all the time. Sometimes it was difficult to remember that not everyone was appreciative of stares, especially when they were trying to relax. And not everyone was gay, of course. Which was an absolute *crime*, as far as he was concerned.

Quiet fell over the sauna and Jonty studied his hooves, frowning at a hairline crack that had appeared on the right one. He needed more hoof oil: hooves were always the one thing that he forgot to care for as regularly as he could. He narrowed his eyes, glaring at them as if the hooves had personally and irrefutably offended him. His tail flicked. Behind, on a higher bench, the crocodile chortled, amusement rasping from his throat.

A few more minutes so I don't look awkward and I can go, he told himself, closing his eyes to enjoy the heat the best he could. *Can always be more careful with staring, it's not that bad a thing to be caught. I'm sure no one minded. It's just a look, a little look.*

His lips turned down sullenly, forehead creasing.

She'll will laugh like a hyena when I tell her I struck out. Again...

Luckily, not everything was down to the sorry colt.

"Seen you around here a bit, horse," the zebra broke the silence, throwing one arm over the next bench up. "You work pretty hard."

The horse stiffened and looked up, ears pricked. A compliment? His heart *glowed*, chest puffing up noticeably.

"I try." Jonty cleared his throat, leaning back in an attempt to appear casual, mimicking the zebra. "I've not seen you here all that much though."

The zebra's ear flicked lazily.

"We only come from time to time." He jerked his head in the direction of his companions. "Local rugby team, get one of the personal trainers on us. It's great to supplement our usual stuff, though we're usually on the pitch or our local gym. Trainer here is too good to pass up on though."

The crocodile rumbled, formidable jaws parted in what Jonty realised a heartbeat later was a reptilian grin. He wondered how the crocodile could walk from place to place without the concern of other furs. Jonty shivered. One snap of those jaws he was certain could take his head clean off his neck and sever any remaining sinew with a twist and a death roll.

If only the thought did not make his cock swell, wickedly slipping from its sheath. The equine swallowed hard, a lump in his throat. Oh, he did so have an inclination towards predators...

"On us? You wish," the crocodile laughed, voice deep and slow. "You couldn't take your eyes off his dick."

The zebra bristled.

"Oh, look who's talking," he huffed with a moist snort, tail thwapping the bench. "You're the one who was in the shower with him. For much longer than necessary to have a shower, might I add."

The lion chuckled and leaned forward, paws dangling as he rested his elbows on his knees.

"Yeah, and we all know what happened in there, don't we?" He shot Jonty a conspirator's wink. "You came out clean in all the right places... Had to get those spots in nice and *deep*, hm?"

Flipping a paw up in what could have been an obscene gesture but was too swift to tell, the crocodile looked away, a smirk snarling down his reptilian snout. The horse, however, could barely contain his excitement, muscles thrumming with sudden, uncontainable energy.

Was it really true? Jonty's heart leapt. Was it just his luck that there were some more gay furs at his gym? More that seemed to be open to fun? If so, could he have stumbled across a better group? Straightening his back, he raised an eyebrow at the zebra, shoulder blades warm against the wood.

"Not got eyes for the ladies then?" He asked, tone casual despite his racing heart. "Thought that's what all the rugby dudes were after – pussy."

The zebra shook his head.

"Nah, the lot of us are gay," he answered. "We tend to stick together. The rest of the blokes on the team are all right but, y'know, it's hard to mesh with everyone if they know what you like and all that. Don't hang out outside training."

"Yeah," the wolf chimed in. "They always think you're looking at their dick. As if! I got higher fucking standards than that."

"Damn straight," the lion added, bobbing his muzzle in agreement.

The zebra paused, looking Jonty over as if seeing him in a new light. The horse squirmed under the scrutiny, spreading his legs to better conceal the bulge in his shorts. Belatedly he wished that he'd gone for a looser pair, something where it would be easier to hide the increasingly obvious bulge.

"Weren't you with a filly at the gym?" He asked, ears flicking off a drop of rapidly cooling sweat.

"Mare," Jonty corrected him automatically: she'd always loathed being called a filly. "And yeah, I was, but we're just friends. Against my will, but friends all the same. She's set me up with a few mates of hers but I'm between boyfriends right now...you could say."

"Oh, so you're gay too." The wolf nodded. "Cool."

"It's actually pretty hot in here."

They laughed lightly, politely, at his joke. Indeed, sweat covered their bodies from the tips of their ears to their tails, though not a single one of them appeared to be in any rush to leave the sauna with friendly company present. The zebra slid closer to Jonty, hissing through his teeth as he skimmed on to a hotter part of the bench, legs casually parted with paws dangling between his thighs. Jonty was suddenly aware that he had never gotten any of their names and a cool shiver thrilled down his spine.

Ignorant to his friend's watchful eyes, the zebra leaned over and rested the palm of his paw, too casually to be accidental, on Jonty's thigh. The horse's skin jumped, twitching in that way that only equines seemed able to master, and he struggled to sit still, paws curling into tight fists, nails digging into his palms. His heart raced, pounding like the beat of a drum to which he could not dance to, and he let out a gasp as the zebra started to stroke his leg gently, allowing the very tips of his fingers to caress his new friend's coat.

To Jonty's embarrassment, his cock slipped from its sheath, swelling into the little space allowed by his tight, fitted shorts. He whickered nervously, wondering whether he should get up and leave, half-rising, though an appreciative murr from the zebra's lips steadied his nerve. The zebra shook his head and, cautiously, Jonty reclaimed his seat, heart pounding with such force that every beat was uncomfortable, on the edge of pain. Just what was going on?

"Easy there, horse," the zebra grinned. "We're not going to do anything to you that you don't want. But you got hard there so quickly for us, it would be a shame to not appreciate a fine, studly colt now, wouldn't it? You came here just for us, didn't you?"

"I...I didn't mean to..."

Jonty blushed, his coltish demeanour vanishing at the paws of the larger, stronger male. Oh, it was so good to be touched, it had been too long. Glancing back, he whinnied, the whites of his eyes showing, as he caught sight of the crocodile, their thick cock in one paw. The reptile parted his jaws and hissed, a roiling, thunderous sound that made Jonty quiver down to his hooves, eyes transfixed upon that massive rod of flesh, a bulbous white head gleaming with pre-cum.

"You don't seem to mind the attention anyway." The zebra's paw travelled higher, teasing over the shape of Jonty's cock, fat shaft showing through his shorts. "Think we're lucky we ran into you, horse... Very lucky indeed."

Jonty huffed and tipped his head back, squirming.

"Ah...you are?"

"*Yes*."

It was the lion who answered, rubbing the back of his paw over the growing bulge in his swim trunks, a low yowl curling from his black tinted lips, rimming a maw crammed with sharp teeth. Once composed enough to talk, he bared those teeth in a grin.

"We've been looking for a new slut to use after practice."

"Slut?" Jonty stiffened, ears flattening to his skull. "I am *not* a slut."

"Really?" The zebra tilted his head. "Because you seem to be rather enjoying this right now. Bet you want a nice, thick cock under your tail, don't you? You want a real stud to mount you, make you sore, *fuck* you."

"No, I don't..." Jonty whinnied, though his protest was weak. "I don't have guys fuck me. That's what I do. I'm not a bottom."

There was no sense of conviction in his words and his statements rang deliciously false in the thick, dry heat. The four companions seemed to cast a spell over him as he looked from one to another, coming to an unspoken agreement. He wriggled on the bench, heat rushing to his cheeks as his cock engorged further, the head straining at the waistband of his shorts, threatening to break free. Damn his sheath! It put the fucking thing in just the right position to threaten his decency! Not that he had much decency left when other furs were working themselves up around him, taking advantage of their timely privacy.

Oh, he *wanted* them: he didn't have to question that for even a heartbeat. Only Jonty was not one to make the first move. He had to be told. Whining, he looked between them, eyes wide and plaintive as his cock throbbed and his ears slipped to the sides submissively.

"We'll set you right, horse, don't you fret." The wolf slipped off the middle bench, standing before the Jonty with his cock out. "Why don't you put those lips to good use, hm?"

The horse shook his head and looked away, though his upper lip quivered out from his muzzle.

"No, I won't do it," he insisted, folding his paws into his lap. "I don't know you. Do you think you can make me?"

"Oh, you will do it," the wolf said, reaching forward to twist his fingers into the horse's mane. "Because if you truly did not want this, you would've already left and not be so fucking turned on, colt."

His eyes narrowed and Jonty's heart skipped a beat, wondering exactly what he was in for as the wolf's lips curled up from his muzzle in a feral snarl.

"Now suck my cock, little slut."

Dragging Jonty's head down by a handful of mane, he gave the poor horse no choice in the matter, pinching the corner of his lips to force his mouth wide open. He wedged the pointed tip of his cock into the stallion's muzzle and thrust in smoothly, making good use of the longer, equine muzzle. In the wolf's opinion, a horse muzzle was perfectly suited to sucking cock, and, despite his weak struggles, Jonty closed his eyes and moaned around the smooth, thick length. The head of Jonty's cock finally broke through his shorts, pushing up against his lower stomach, and the zebra whistled, looking it over appreciatively.

The horse gagged as the wolf's cock pushed to the back of his throat, making his body jerk instinctively, fighting the urge to cough, to gag and to hack. He swallowed with difficulty, salty pre-cum oozing viscously down his throat, and allowed the wolf to pull him forward, thrusting him to his knees. Saliva drooled from Jonty's muzzle, his body striving to compensate for the dry, stifling room. He could already feel his head going fuzzy, tail sticking to his legs from the sheer volume of sweat pouring down him.

Squeezing Jonty's ears, the wolf groaned, savouring the sensation of a young muzzle around his member, the knot half-swollen as he thrust. The slick shaft slid over Jonty's tongue as he sucked, paws on the wolf's legs as the he guided him back and forth, bucking into his muzzle with enough force to make his balls slap into the horse's chin. He shuddered, fingers curling into those wide, muscled thighs, and flipped his tail up, rump thrusting back as he imagined being filled, fucked, as he was sucking the wolf off. But that would only happen if his new friends so chose. He was just a toy in their paws and welcoming every second of it.

The wolf barked sharply, the sound echoing around the small, enclosed room. His thrusts came more urgently, each breath arriving with the heave of his chest, shorts slinking down the curve of his ass, giving his friend an unintentional, yet appreciated show. Jonty's nostrils flared and the horse suckled feverishly, desperate to feel the hot spill of seed down his throat. He had sucked enough cock to know that the wolf was close and, oh, how he wanted to be used, his muzzle but a place for them to spend their seed, as much as they had to give. Grunting, he panted with an open muzzle, tail wagging furiously as orgasm approached, knot swelling outside Jonty's lips in anticipation.

The zebra chuckled and shook his head, edging in closer for a better view of the action, resting on one arm as he stretched out. Whining, the wolf thrust rapidly, hips moving like a jack hammer as he struggled to hold back, to draw out the pleasure for a few seconds longer, just a bit more. Jonty strained to contain the fat length, knot pressing upon his lips as he whinnied, nostrils flaring, and the wolf grunted.

"Getting off so soon, are you?" The wolf's lion friend mocked, a barbed cock in his own paw.

"Mmmph," he snorted, caught between lust and indignation. "Fuck no. But this little bitch won't take the heat if I don't cum soon."

Jonty shuddered. He was right, as wrong as he wanted the wolf to be. The heat of the sauna made his mouth dry and his head swim. His tail clung to his legs, soaked with sweat, and he closed his eyes, suffering willingly in silence as the wolf thrust three more times, pinched the horse's ears and ejaculated with a howl.

"Honestly." The crocodile rolled his eyes. "Do you want the whole fucking gym to hear you?"

"Yeah..." The wolf panted. "You're right. We wouldn't want to share our new slut now, would we?"

Jonty flinched, swallowing his mouthful of cum and licking it from his lips, paws resting upon his own thighs again. As the wolf drew away, he felt another paw on his head and looked up to see the lion standing over him, long tail lashing. Fingers curled into his hair, drawing it painfully tight, and Jonty groaned.

"Come with us, colt."

With his fingers wound into Jonty's mane, the lion tugged him after, gentler than the wolf had been in kind. Jonty licked dry lips, swallowing what semen was left in his muzzle, and followed helplessly, hard cock bobbing as he went. Briefly he was thankful that it was late enough on a Sunday that most gym patrons had left for the day for families and other pursuits. Either way, he had heard that the coaches at the gym liked indulging, so to speak, much as he had heard about that crocodile's experience. He had nothing to worry about regarding discovery. All was well. Absolutely everything would be okay...

Or would it? What if he was discovered, ass up in the locker room? What would another – yet another stranger! – do to him? The thought made Jonty shiver, imagining a string of furs, one after the other, coming upon him in his vulnerable state and taking their turns.

He still did not know their names as they shoved him into the showers, crowding him into a corner with predatory grins. The zebra nickered and stomped a hoof, black cock bobbing.

"In with you!"

Tossing the horse gently into the spacious communal shower, the lion grinned. The showers were automatic and the nearest immediately set off by Jonty's body, dousing him in a cool stream of water. Gasping, he turned his muzzle upwards and parted his lips, allowing the thin streams to pour into his mouth. Though it was not much, it soothed his parched lips and cooled his forehead, easing the burn of the sauna. His head spun and he slowly returned to himself, lowering himself to his knees, water streaming over his head, neck and down his back.

"Eager to get on your knees, I see," the lion said, strutting in, cock erect. "I like a keen one."

Eyeing the lion's legs, pacing closer, the horse's hooves scuffed lightly over the shower tiles. The shower flattened his mane to his neck where it clung in a wet arch and the lion ran his fingers through it, claws scratching a line down his neck. Whickering, he arched into the touch, cock hard between his spread thighs.

"Up." He ordered. "My cock is not meant for your lips. I have a tastier treat in mind for myself."

"Such language..." The zebra chuckled, leaning against the wall. "I wouldn't expect such uncouth behaviour from *you*."

"Oh, shut up, you cock."

Snorting, Jonty clambered to his hooves, struggling to find purchase on the tiles. The lion spun him around and pinned him to the wall, shoving the horse's chest flat against it. Water ran down his back and over his rump and the lion's lips quirked in a smirk as he lifted the damp strands of his tail out of the way to expose a tight pucker of a tail hole. Jonty's tail hole winked as if he was a mare in season and the lion purred, squeezing a digit into the inviting hole. Digging his teeth into his lower lip, Jonty shuddered and pushed back, pressing both of his paws flat on the wall for leverage.

"Needy little horse... Wanting more than a finger, hm?"

Jonty groaned and nodded, muzzle bobbing several times in swift succession. The lion pressed his paw between his shoulder blades and held him to the wall, pushing forward enough for his barbed cock to rub over the equine's backside.

"Chuck me the shampoo, would ya? It's all this colt's gonna get."

A bottle landed in his open paw and he squirted a liberal helping of it on to Jonty's tail hole, rubbing it in and sliding two fingers inside with the aid of the slick, viscous gel.

"Get ready, pony..."

Two paws landed on Jonty's shoulders and, without any need for a guiding paw, the lion eased the tip of his tapered cock under the equine's tail. He thrust inside in one smooth motion and hissed, jaws parted in a feral expression of pleasure, muzzle contorted. Jonty gasped for breath as he was filled and pushed back, the lion's hips flush with his rump, only to start when the lion withdrew, barbs catching and pulling within his passage. In a female of his species, the barbs would have induced ovulation, but, in his case, they raked, causing equal amounts of pleasure and pain. In the initial moment, Jonty could not have said which one proved more dominant.

He groaned as the lion thrust, claiming him with savage need. The lion grabbed a lock of Jonty's forelock and he dragged the horse's head back savagely, hips powering forward brutally. The feline rasped his tongue over the side of Jonty's neck, pushing around to clasp his teeth around the horse's throat. Jonty shuddered bodily, buttocks clenching as he suffered through the thrusts, the drag of pain. He had no choice in the matter with such a predator overpowering him. What chance did a horse have against a lion? A predator? He could sink his teeth into his rump any time he pleased! Jonty trembled.

Whinnying, Jonty found some purchase on the wall and bucked, hooves skittering wildly. The lion roared, jaws parting ferociously, the vibrations rumbling through Jonty's throat, making him intimately aware of the feline's power. The cat thrust like a being possessed, pummelling the horse's tail hole so viciously that Jonty wondered if he would return to his normal tightness that he was so renowned for by the game patrons. Sure it would be worth it for one liaison...right? The groaned and pressed his forehead to the wall, cool seeping into his skull. How long had it been since the lion had got off? It was not going to be much longer if the lion had his way.

He did not hear the slap of the crocodile's large feet – they could not be called paws – in the shower room. The first indication he had that anything had changed was the feeling of being hauled bodily away from the wall and deposited on his paws and knees, lion cock still shoved deep under his tail. The crocodile stood before him with a grin that displayed each and every one of his deadly teeth, designed to grip and tear, silencing his hapless prey forever. Digging his claws into Jonty's hips, the lion growled, warning him to stay still, and Jonty pushed his rump back, tail flicking against the lion's side. Oh no – he was not going *anywhere*.

Taking his pale cock in one paw, the crocodile knelt and rubbed it along the side of Jonty's muzzle, smearing a long, clear stream of pre-cum over his coat. It was washed away a second later by the stream of water but Jonty groaned, submitting to the intimate marking. The crocodile smirked and pressed the tip of his cock to the horse's lips, waiting for the pony to open up for him. There was no force needed and Jonty blinked up at his top through a sodden forelock, splattered across his forehead.

"Suck it, bitch."

Jonty parted his lips eagerly and subsequently gagged as the crocodile took the invitation in the span of a split second, thrusting deep into his elongated, equine muzzle. The bulb at the head tickled the back of the horse's throat and Jonty convulsed, struggling to breathe until the crocodile withdrew, only to thrust again with greater force. He hissed viciously, eyes closed as he leaned back against the wall, enjoying the cool upon his skin while a hot muzzle wrapped around his dick.

The lion powered into his rump, sinking his claws in a little deeper from time to time just to see his prey for the evening squirm and buck. The edge of pain made Jonty snort like a wild stallion, tail hole clenching wickedly upon the rogue shaft to the point where the lion could hardly move. He chuffed softly and leaned over the horse, admiring the lines of muscle in his back, engorged from his own workout. They were lucky to find such an eager slut as a specimen to fuck. If they were even luckier, they could arrange a regular time to meet and fill the colt with cum. Licking his lips, he imagined coming home from work to cum all over the pretty horse's muzzle while another of his friends – it didn't matter which – reamed his ass, spilling a nice, thick load into his slutty rump.

Jonty moaned around the shaft between his lips, expertly rubbing his tongue against the underside with each roll of the crocodile's hips. His own length slapped and jerked beneath his stomach, the mottled length evading the restraint of his shorts and sending spurts of pre-cum down the drain. He was dangerously close to cumming, every one of the lion's thrusts slamming into his prostate and rocking him on to the reptile's cock, forcing his muzzle forward so that he took the length deeper and deeper. Yet the crocodile was not satisfied with his efforts.

"Come on, little pony," the crocodile grunted, grasping a handful of his mane to drag his muzzle down on his cock. "Give a proper deep-throat, hey? Or are your skills off today?"

Jonty tried to shake his head but the paw in his hair kept him firmly in place. Instead, his eyes hardened and he slid his lips down the length of the croc's cock, eyes widening, until his velvety muzzle met the hard hide of crocodilian abdomen.

"Mmm..." The reptile groaned, letting his head fall back, the top of his skull perpendicular to the wall. "Better... Better. Keep that up, slut."

The lion snarled and dragged his claws down Jonty's back, raising four red lines of blood – scratches at worst – the horse twitching at the spark of pain. The water splashed with red as the lion lost control, hammering into the tight rump with the drive of a feline possessed, feral need overruling any concern he may have had for the equine. As the lion's lusts rose and rose, the crocodile rammed his cock down Jonty's throat, using his muzzle as nothing more than a cock sleeve and a dumping ground for his cum. Showing his anthro heritage, a steady stream of pre-cum drooled down Jonty's throat from the croc', thick and viscous. Though the two abusing his body grew ever closer to cumming, Jonty was left denied, the stimulation not quite enough to rock him over the edge, only teeter, wanting and waiting and whimpering.

The crocodile ground his teeth together abruptly and parted his jaws in a roiling, feral hiss that sent a chill down Jonty's spine a second before cum poured down his throat in a thick torrent. Jonty arched, grinding his rump back and gulped quickly, though not swiftly enough to catch every drop of seed as the crocodile thrust wildly. Cum dripped from the strained corners of his mouth and Jonty's eyes grew wide, own cock throbbing as it begged for a release that was not soon to be had. Not far behind the crocodile was the lion who roared loud enough to send vibrations through the floor and walls – surely raising the curiosity of some of the other gym patrons – barbed cock throbbing as he emptied his balls under Jonty's tail.

With a low groan, the crocodile withdrew his cock from the slut's mouth. Rather than softening, it remained firm as it was sucked back into its sheath, permanently erect within the crocodile's lower abdomen. He grinned as he patted Jonty condescendingly upon the head, laughing at his attempts to regain breath, throat sore from the pounding he had been given. The lads were not gentle on him – he could not lie. Yet that roughness was all he craved. The crocodile paced away, feet slapping the floor, and gave the grinning zebra a high five as he passed, rumbling a laugh to no one in particular. Jonty wondered if he knew that he had forgotten his sauna shorts, bundled up in a corner of the shower room.

The lion ran his fingers through Jonty's mane and the horse rolled his hips back, tail lifted high and begging for more. He chuckled, rubbing the patch of skin right under the base of the horse's tail until he quivered.

"Mmmph, not bad, pony," he panted, chest heaving as he struggled for breath. "Maybe we'll be seeing you again, hey?"

Jonty hoped so, yet he still groaned when the lion pulled his softening cock from his rump, marking the horse with a smear of his seed. The horse was glad to see no blood when he ducked his muzzle down to check between his legs, though there was one left unsatisfied in the room and a wolf with a paw squeezing his knot panting in the corner. Eyes fixed on his equine prey, the wolf stalked forward, eager to take his turn on Jonty's muzzle once more. But the needy equine needed more than a cock stuffing his maw: he needed a dick under his tail. Something to claim him, let him know that he was truly and utterly used.

His cock throbbed, pulsing.

Cum dripping from his tail hole, Jonty panted heavily and looked back over his shoulder to the one left unattended, flagging his tail up in open invitation. The zebra murred and pushed himself up off the wall, cock in his paw, as the slut thrust his rump back wantonly. One was not enough. He had to be filled over and over again, or else he would never be satisfied. Shamefully, Jonty dipped his muzzle down to the damp floor and raised his ass higher, cum oozing down the back of his thighs and pucker winking.

"Please fuck me..."

His time there was not over, but he had to take it all smoothly, patiently. Like his friend, the mare, always said, he had to pace himself.

With the wolf and the zebra however to double team him until he was a mess of drooling cock on the shower floor, Jonty may well have bitten off more than he could chew.

As their newest "sauna slut," however, he didn't care one bit.

Personal Training

"So! You're here for a personal training session."

The lithe otter gulped and stood up straighter, shifting from hind paw to paw. He had little to no muscle – typical of otters – and his brown eyes darted fervently from left to right as if keeping track of any and all possible exits. He would not want to be trapped, despite voluntarily taking himself to the gym. It was a scary environment to a little fur, after all, with clanging weights and grunting lifters, sprinters puffing on the treadmills. The otter licked his lips, chest rising and falling too quickly for him to be relaxed.

Dressed in black gym shorts with a white, vertical stripe and a plain green T-shirt, he could have fitted in easily to the strength and body building focused gym. There were smaller types, slimmer furs, there working on sports fitness and the group included several otters competing in swimming. To him, however, the clothing was uncomfortable and he tugged at the waistband of his shorts, scrambling for the courage to speak up as he had said he would. He'd made himself a promise.

"Y-yes, I am," he mumbled, avoiding eye contact with the bull behind the desk. "I'm here to sign up. Today. Well...now."

The black bull studied him with a jauntily angled muzzle as his moist nostrils flared and he pushed a clipboard across the desk to the otter. Picking up the pen with a paw that trembled faintly, he signed his name with a flourish, lifting the tail on the end of the 'y' in a flirty flick. Tilting his head to read upside down, the bull's lips twitched and he flicked his ropey tail against the counter with a thwack that made the otter jump, eyes wide.

"Ronny, it is then. You been here before?"

The otter shook his head, scuffing the sole of one brand new trainer over the toe of the other.

"Nope... First time."

"You been to a gym before?" He pressed.

"*Daily Exercise*, just that one."

The otter flushed, wondering if his choice of gym was going to be judged, but the bull made no comment, though he did raise an eyebrow.

"And what name do you prefer to go by? Ronny? Ronald?"

Swallowing, the otter smiled sheepishly.

"Ronny is fine, most people call me that."

Feeling the otter start to come out of his shell, the bull smiled and kindly offered him his paw to shake, licking his moist nose with a very pink tongue.

"Awesome. Name's Cormac. Shall we get started?"

Nodding, Ronny chanced a smile and followed the bull with his eyes as the larger male stepped around the counter, leaving a frowning lion to take care of the desk. Cormac scratched his thick neck and surreptitiously looked the otter up and down, taking his measure out of the corner of his eye.

Before they leapt into something beyond what the otter was looking for, Cormac paused by the elliptical machines – of which there were only two – both of which were unoccupied.

"So, what's your goal here?" He questioned, fingers tucked into his pockets as he rocked back on his cloven hooves.

Pursing his lips, Ronny's gaze slid to the left as he considered the question, wondering what exactly he was doing in the gym in the first place.

"Just general fitness," Ronny coughed, looking down at the padded floor, which was covered from wall to wall in Olympic matting. "It's a New Year's resolution kind of thing."

Cormac tried not to smirk, brown eyes widening just a fraction as he swallowed a smart retort that would not have been wise around clientele.

"Well, we get a few of those in here," the bull acknowledged with a barely perceptible roll of his eyes that he kindly hid from Ronny. "It'll take a lot of hard work and it won't happen overnight but you shouldn't be discouraged by that."

"It takes a long time..." Ronny sighed and looked down, twisting his paws together. "What if nothing happens?"

"What do you mean by that?"

"I like to see changes," he said simply. "I work in IT and, if there are any bugs, I like to iron them out. Everything has to be right."

Ears flicking amongst the clamour of metal on metal and grunts of males and females alike working out in the gym, the bull edged closer. He expected the typical New Year's resolutioner that wanted to either be buff in no time – drugs or enhancements non-optional – or tone up a little, as the saying went. There was something different about this one, however, a real edge that perked Cormac's interest more than the daft antics of most newbies. Though Ronny's nose twitched distastefully at the clean scent of sweat emanating through the gym, Cormac figured that maybe, just maybe, he would be able to train the shy otter.

Every fur had a weakness. Or a motivating point.

"Let's get you started on a fun routine for general fitness then," Cormac said, folding his arms across his broad chest, gym branded shirt straining over muscle. "Hop up on the elliptical, one foot on each side."

Awkwardly, the otter nodded and jumped up on the large, flat pedals, one for each of his hind paws. His rudder swung and slapped the backs of his thighs as the paw rests moved and he reached for the rods for his forepaws instinctively, feeling safer with something to hold on to.

"A good way to get yourself in the zone is to start with some light cardio," Cormac explained as the otter slowly started to work on the elliptical, cautiously at first and then with increasing confidence. "It won't be your whole session but it's good to get yourself into a rhythm and it's easy to start off, not threatening."

Though his stride was short and choppy, the otter settled into a light jog. As the elliptical did not move a fixed distance like some machines, the amount of pressure he put on the paw pads allowed him to lengthen or shorten his stride to whatever was comfortable without putting undue strain on his body. Cormac's eyes roamed his body as the otter found his stride, stepping out more confidently even as his eyes darted around the gym, passing over each and every single gym client in sight. The bull frowned, darker lips turning down at the corners. Not a single fur had their eyes on the otter, no matter what his nerves, or whatever it was, told him.

Time to regain his focus.

"Let's dial it up a notch, shall we? You're breezing your way through this."

Perhaps a higher intensity would better claim the otter's attention. Tapping the machine twice, Cormac increased the resistance, forcing Ronny to work harder. Looking straight ahead of him, the otter opened his mouth and panted softly, the pulse monitor built into the handles of the machine tracking its subsequent increase. The bull studied him, fingers curled around the underside of his jaw. Interesting.

"You don't like thinking that other people are watching you, hm?"

The otter flushed and shook his head, deigning to answer verbally as his heart pounded, muscles complaining as they were forced to complete a motion at an intensity that his body was not used to.

"Don't you swim?" Cormac probed. "Sorry if that's a bit of a generalisation but you *are* an otter."

The otter huffed for breath, paws sweaty on the handles of the elliptical as he pedalled. His pace was great enough that it had become difficult for a relatively unfit fur to talk and pedal, lungs working hard.

"Yeah..." He swallowed loudly, muzzle tipping back to show the pulse in his throat as he struggled to talk and pedal at the same time. "It's...different. In the...water. No...stress. Just fun."

Cormac nodded, though he wondered what was so different about swimming. It was exercise too, wasn't it? And the otter would wear less clothing to go to the pool to swim. It didn't make sense but it didn't have to make sense for him to be able to work with his new client. And if wandering eyes were such a problem, Cormac had one solution to try. It was all a process of trial and error with new clients anyway.

The bull only thought this method may be more entertaining for the two of them.

"All right, enough of that," the bull instructed, tapping the side of the machine to draw Ronny's attention. "Slow it down yourself."

Bobbing his small muzzle, Ronny obligingly slowed his steps, dialling down the intensity until he could have been walking with a relaxed, if unusual, stride, arms swinging along with the handles of the elliptical. When he stood still, only rocking slightly back and forth, he looked to the bull for guidance, eyes dropping and then darting up against guiltily. He couldn't look at any of the other gym patrons, even though a curious gazelle cast him a look for standing on the machine rather than using it. Cormac smiled, catching the otter's stare: bingo.

"Right, hop off, we're going somewhere different."

Cormac turned on his heel and beckoned the otter to follow him with a casual flip of his paw, rump curved through the fabric of his jogging bottoms. It was good to be able to wear comfortable clothes at the gym, he thought, as he glanced back just the once to check Ronny was following him. Time to play to the otter's liking, as it were.

"I'm using the small room, okay?" He called down to the front desk, striding away without waiting for a response.

Ronny trotted to catch up, trainers slapping the floor, and grumbled at the light ache already tingling through his legs. Swimming was never that difficult! Spreading the energy for swimming across his whole body and, as an otter, he was naturally attuned to it. It was easy for him, as little as he enjoyed the pool those days. His eyes would wander as much as he feared there would be other eyes on him. Swallowing, he trailed his gaze down his personal trainer's back to where his tail swung with the motion of his body. The bull's ass was impossible to ignore and Ronny could only imagine the years of work that had gone into such a physique.

He blushed, finding it ironic that, though he did not enjoy having eyes upon him, he looked more than was strictly polite. It was an odd conundrum and one that he had berated himself for many, many times. Still, he could not bring himself to drag his gaze away from the bull's tight rump and the hypnotic swing of his tail. He wondered what that backside would feel like under his paw...

Ronny gulped, rubbing his throat, and pushed the thoughts from his mind. Those ideas were not why he was in the gym.

Taking Ronny through a room set with half racks and barbells, the bull continued on to a door set in the side of the main room. The room was simply set up with Olympic matting on the floor with enough space for a fur to complete a variety of exercises in relative solitude. There were no windows and a small stereo was seated in the corner of the room, ready for use. A single barbell leaned against the far wall with a variety of weight plates racked neatly on a stand, demonstrating that the room was mainly for use with free weight. Not a single, comforting machine was in sight.

Closing the door, Ronny took in the room.

"Why are we in here?" He asked, eyes rising to the pull up bar set a little distance up, bolted into opposite walls. "What about the other stuff?"

"It's a little more private," Cormac said, evading the direct question he best he could in the moment: it would not do to give too much away right up front. "You don't like other people looking at you, right? Isn't that why you're acting like a cornered fur at gunpoint."

The otter heaved a sigh and nodded, looking down at the floor. The grey matting was flecked with flakes of black, drawing the eye from spot to spot as if it would never quite settle.

"No, I don't, but I guess that much is obvious if you picked up on it already. Sorry."

Cormac clapped him on the shoulder and shook his head, smile as broad as ever.

"Don't be sorry! Now, let us be on with it, there's no sense in holding off your session any longer. You want to get the full service we provide, of course."

Ronny gave the tiniest of smiles and nodded, standing to attention as the bull slid a ten-kilo plate on to each end of the barbell.

"This should be easy enough for you," he said, stepping away without adding clamps to keep the plates in place. "Don't worry about the weight, I just want to run you through a standard barbell row. It's a training bar, so more flexible than the Olympic bars..."

Ronny nodded, eyes glazing over as he strove to mentally log every scrap of information he was given, though much of it went over the poor otter's head. He smiled in a way that he hoped conveyed that he understood at least enough of the bull's words and, under direction, stepped up to the barbell, sliding his hips back so his body was low enough to collect the bar from the ground. It was raised high enough by the plates that he could take it in an overhand grip, bending his legs to slip down comfortably low.

In a true Pendlay row, he took the weight in his paws and Cormac touched the middle of his back, reminding him to keep it flat and steady, as the otter pulled the weight towards his body, triceps pointing up. The bar wobbled and the otter's muzzle twisted in concentration as he lowered it to the padded floor again, only to lift it in a smoother, cleaner motion under the bull's encouragement. A plate slipped and Ronny muttered his annoyance under his breath, though his words did not yet curl into a curse. Cormac smoothed over his frown and moved in to assist.

"Right, a bit wonky but you're using the right muscles,"

Guiding him through a series of light exercises, using the barbell and neatly racked dumbbells from the corner of the room, the bull smiled, his eyes warming to the otter's determination. Without curious eyes on him, or the implication of such, he took willingly to

Cormac's education until every muscle in his body was slick and warm, moving freely and ready to work. The bull flicked his tail and scratched the underside of his jaw, blunt finger-hooves rasping through the short stubble there.

"I think we'll have you started on a basic squat now, with weight," he said in reference to the bodyweight squats he had run the otter through to warm-up, a portion of their time already disappeared. "We have no squat rack in here, so I'll lend a paw. Stand up."

Removing the weight from the bar, Cormac easily lifted it up to the level of the shorter otter's shoulders and showed him how to rest it on his traps, paws curling comfortably around the cool metal. At ten kilos – or so Cormac had told him – it didn't feel like he had any weight there at all and he more confidently than earlier dropped into a low squat, going past the point where his thighs would have been parallel. Back flat and steady, he rose cleanly and continued the motion for a full, simple set of ten repetitions. The bull rolled his shoulders backwards.

"Too easy, more weight for that one, otter."

Removing the bar from Ronny's paws, Cormac quickly slid two weight plates on to either end of the bar – something to provide his trainee with a greater challenge, lest he become complacent. Besides, the bull thought as he concealed his smirk with a meticulously painted on smile, he wanted to have to step in to help the otter. That was part of the plan, the deal.

With greater weight on the bar, Ronny found himself struggling as he dropped his body into the first squat. The bull eased in, palms beneath the bar to guide it as he spread his legs, not taking the weight from the otter but giving him the confidence he needed in order to rise through the lift, if lacking his original steadiness. As he supported the otter, Cormac shifted closer, crotch brushing against the seat of Ronny's gym trousers. The otter jerked, bar swaying.

"*What* are you doing?"

The otter squeaked, hips rocking back away from the bull's abdomen as if he had been stung. Blinking with false innocence, the bull flicked his tail and lowered a paw to the otter's hip, shifting his rump further back in the semblance of adjusting his form a little too intimately for comfort. Ronny's heart raced, blood roaring in his ears.

"*Encouragement.*"

Cormac grinned, dropping the otter a conspirator's wink as he followed Ronny, tail thumping lightly against the otter's leg. Trembling, the otter bent forward at his hips and pushed his body through the exercise again, the barbell supported across the tops of his shoulders. The near sexual nature of the exercised was emphasised as he pushed his rump back, hinging at the hips, yet he did not put the barbell down or demand that Cormac give him more space. Ronny's blood sang as the bull closed in even further, body moving fluidly with his so that his form was supported and not interrupted in the slightest.

"Is this private enough for you, Ronny?" The bull breathed in his ear, his breath a hot wash across the otter's coat. "No eyes on you here... Just mine."

The otter squeaked, rudder slapping Cormac's thigh and completed a shaky eighth rep, form juddering. Taking the bar from the otter, Cormac set it down as the otter took a brief break, heart thudding so hard he feared it would burst right out of his chest to continue beating on the mats. His respite was short lived, however, and the barbell was soon resting across his traps again with the larger, stronger bull easing in closer than ever to him. Sweat dampening a line across his brow, the otter surprised himself with a grunt as he sank lower, the bull murmuring his approval in his ear.

"Excellent... One more set. Ten reps. *Go.*"

He didn't need to raise his voice for Ronny to take note and the otter looked straight ahead as he pushed, doing his best to ignore the bulge grinding into his rump. The bull had to know what he was doing! It *had* to be intentional. Blood roared in Ronny's ears as he forced his body through the motion, air ripping from his lungs as he fought to control his breath. And all while the bull's blunt fingertips were there supporting the bar ever so slightly as his form steadied his position, crotch pushing Ronny's thick tail aside.

There could be no accident about it.

Form wavering on his final repetition, Ronny groaned as his drove the bar up, tongue lolling from his muzzle as if he had suddenly turned into a canine. The otter heaved a sigh as the bull took the weight from him, angling his hips away as if he even had the slightest hope of hiding the bulge in his jogging bottoms from the eagle-eyed Cormac. The bull's ropey tail slapped his calf and he grunted approvingly.

"You can increase the weight on that one next time," Cormac commented, taking the barbell from the otter's shoulders and placing it gently upon the matted floor. "Use the rack. It'll be around others, but you need it to get the weight up in place. Make sure you're getting your hips back nice and far though...like you want me to fuck you."

Ronny squirmed as the bull eyed him levelly, gaze raking his body with a tight air. He wasn't just approving the otter's form this time – it was much more than that. Ronny shifted his weight from hind paw to paw, edging away until his shoulder brushed the wall, just for a little distance in the otherwise confining space. He laughed, sound ringing hollow, as if he could take Cormac's comment as a joke. How was he supposed to respond to that? Was there *any* way to respond?

The bull scratched his nose and grinned at the otter, flashing his blunt, grazing teeth.

"But that's what you really want, isn't it otter?" He raised an eyebrow, smirking. "You want me to fuck you."

"No!" Ronny shook his head and held up his paws, attempting a disgusted expression as panic fluttered in his chest. "What the hell are you on about? You were just s-spotting me, right? That's what it's called, isn't it?"

"Yeah...spotting..." Cormac rolled his eyes. "If you didn't like it, then I'm not sure what a trainer like me is supposed to think. You have an obvious hard-on for me, otter-boy."

Ronny bristled, though there was no hiding it. The front of his trousers tented out proudly and wouldn't go down no matter what he thought of. Damn thing... Ronny swore he was the unluckiest otter alive and surreptitiously adjusted the front of his jogging bottoms as if he could more readily cover the bulge. It did him no good at all.

"What male wouldn't react to being treated like that?" He huffed, petulantly folding his arms in front of his chest. "Your cock was practically in my ass! What did you expect me to do? Who wouldn't get an erection there?"

Cormac chuckled deep in his throat.

"Certainly not a *straight* one."

Ronny's jaw fell open and he shook his head wordlessly. He blushed and covered his crotch with one paw, pointedly looking away as his thoughts raced more swiftly than his thudding heart, pounding behind his ribcage. Exercise hurt less than this humiliation! Stifling a groan, the otter kept his eyes carefully averted, frozen in place and burning from head to toe. Even his tail was still. How had the bull known he was gay? Would he have known he was gay if he had moved away from the support in the squat – Cormac's spotting assistance? Ronny screwed up his muzzle, no longer caring what the bull would or wouldn't think of him – already too freaking late for thoughts like that. He growled inwardly, cursing himself in words that he would not dare utter aloud. And the whole matter would have been a lot easier if he wasn't so turned on. Could the bull be interested in him? He didn't dare to hope.

The bull, on the other hoof, had a different perspective to the shy little thing and cast him a look of yearning that Ronny, looking away, would never see. But he didn't have to, not this time. Cormac would make the steps he was too shy to take.

Advancing, Cormac's eyes crinkled in the corners. Training could wait for another day. Something told him that he would have all the time in the world with the otter soon enough. He leaned in close, bending down so that he was almost nose to nose with his charge, a moist muzzle huffing over a smaller, more delicate one. Ronny quivered, tail slapping.

"Want some training, otter? I'll give you a free session on top of this one if you do one thing for me, just one little thing." Cormac winked. "Do you think you can do that for me? Just this one, little thing?"

Resisting the urge to step away from the bull, whose breath washed over his muzzle, Ronny tilted his head far back to look him in the eye and wished he was a foot or so taller. Every muscle in his body thrummed with nervous tension and he curled one paw into a fist as if to use it as a fragile weapon, though it would do no good against his personal trainer. A punch to the bull would be as ineffective as hitting a brick wall without building some strength behind it.

"One thing?" Ronny swallowed, the lump remaining in his throat. "What? What do you want me to do?"

"Get me off, otter. I'm sure a young thing like you can show a bull a good time." He winked lecherously, sliding his paws down to Ronny's hips. "You've been staring at me enough. It doesn't take a genius to figure out what you're after. Or what I'm after. I want your muzzle on my cock, otter."

"Isn't that rather...ah...forward?" Ronny yelped as the bull's paw dipped between his thighs, squeezing his bulge without any node of shame. "What... Do you do this with all your clients? Get them to...mmm..." He groaned against his will, the bull's paw rubbing over his hard-on. "Get them to blow you?"

Cormac tipped his muzzle up to kiss his lips lightly, tongue brushing over them for the briefest of instances.

"Only the special ones."

Easing his paw round to the back of the otter's neck, Cormac pulled him in sharply, pressing his lips to the otter's in a deeper, fiercer kiss. His tongue invaded the smaller otter's muzzle and he curved his paw around the small of Ronny's back as the otter melted into the embrace, body and baser mind responding even as he reacted. It was foolish, absolutely insane! He shouldn't be so easy to handle, easy to manipulate, for he would do as the bull asked in a heartbeat or less. His cock drooled pre-cum into his underwear and the otter shifted uncomfortably, half-reaching to his crotch as if to tug the offending article of clothing – so constricting! – out of the way entirely. He blushed and withdrew his paw, focusing on the kiss that he had no will to escape from even as his mind battled with his better rationality. Screw the sensible!

If it was so wrong, he couldn't understand why it was simultaneously so easy to go along with. He wanted the bull, even if he could not admit it to himself.

Ronny did not have to admit it. Breaking the kiss with a wet snort, Cormac's eyes latched on to his, staring him down until the otter whimpered and slid his gaze down, rounded ears tucked back closer to his skull, though they could not be pinned completely flat. With a smile especially for the otter, Cormac place a heavy paw on his shoulder and levered him down to the matted floor, the otter collapsing to his knees. The bulls thighs swelled before his muzzle and Ronny gasped upon being confronted with their size. He couldn't stop himself from trailing both palms across those thighs, marvelling at their mass and expanse. How many gruelling hours had Cormac devoted to training in order to secure such a physique? Ronny bit his lip, cock throbbing.

Dedication was *hot*.

Cormac pulled down his jogging bottoms, elastic stretching in an easy release for his cock and balls. The heavy bull shaft flopped out of the fabric in Ronny's muzzle and the otter started; the bull wasn't wearing any underwear. Figured. He shuffled back on his heels, settling his body into a crouch, and tried not to think too much about what he was doing. It was madness, absolute and utter madness. And, if he understood that he was mad, perhaps it was all okay to go ahead with what he was doing. The otter shook his head, wondering at his own nerve. Just where had that come from?

Cupping the bull's shaft in his paw, Ronny tentatively licked the head, thick and fleshy and smooth under his tongue. There was a weight to the shaft – it put his to shame – and Ronny squirmed, hopelessly outclassed. Though he hoped the bull would not ask him to take off his gym trousers. Or would the humiliation make him squirm all the more? Flushing hotly, Ronny no longer knew and took the head of Cormac's dick between his lips, suckling lightly on the tip, just to try it. It was all just for fun, he reminded himself, as it hardened in his muzzle.

Cormac stomped, tail lashing, and mooed lowly.

"Good..." The bull murmured, licking his lips with a fat, wet tongue. "Seems like you've done this before, otter."

Instead of feeling embarrassed, Ronny wondered what that tongue would feel like inside him. He leaned in to run his tongue up the underside of the bull's only half-hard length, feeling it firm up within his grip. The bull had not showered in some time – likely not since he had begun his day – and heady musk hit Ronny in the face as his muzzle quested lower. He was hardly dissuaded, however, and only held down a low moan as he lavished attention over Cormac's lightly furred balls, a short coat of downy fur covering both. It was a far cry from the leathery sacks he had seen in pornos and he couldn't say that he disliked it. Ronny opened his mouth wide, suckling on one as his eyes near rolled back into his head.

Breath coming in short, sharp pants, Ronny drew back and took the tip into his mouth for a second time, this time eyes narrowed in inner resolve. His tail slapped the mats and he brought his paws up to the bull's thighs, fingers curling into bare, revealed muscle, and pushed his muzzle down the shaft. It stretched his lips into a tight O-shape and the otter's eyes watered as he eased down, heart thudding painfully. He didn't want to guess at the size for he feared thinking about it for more than the briefest of seconds would intimidate him. He just wanted it in his muzzle, to feel the bull's cream pouring down his throat.

As the head nuzzled into the back of Ronny's throat, the bull lifted a hoof, jigging it in the air with a huff from flared nostrils. Finding his limit, the otter squeezed the bull's nuts gently in one paw and bobbed his muzzle slowly, getting a feel for the motion again. It had been so long since he had sucked a real cock. Maybe that's why he was so eager to drop to his knees for the bull? Ronny didn't care. He chirped happily, though the sound was muffled, as he nudged his tongue up against the underside of the bull's cock, drawing his muzzle back and forth in the best blowjob he was able to give. Pre-cum oozed on to his tongue and the otter eagerly gulped it down, playing his tongue over the slit at the head of Cormac's cock in an unspoken plead for more, always more. He was not an otter to be easily satisfied as simple as his desires were.

In his trousers, his cock drooled enough pre-cum to soak through his jogging bottoms, though the otter was too preoccupied to be worried about how he was going to field off awkward questions from the stain later, sneaking out of the gym. He bucked his hips, imagining another was beneath him with his lips wrapped around Ronny's cock, sucking as desperately as the otter found himself doing. Giving a muffled moan, the otter scrabbled at the bull's thigh, begging for his cum as he mimicked the thrusts he knew Cormac could deliver, pulling his hips up to his crotch as he hammered under the otter's tail. Ronny groaned. Yet he still did not take the full length into his muzzle: he'd reached his limit.

But the bull wasn't going to be satisfied with that – not a chance!

"Mmm..." The bull groaned, rolling his head so that his horns tapped the wall. "Deeper. I know you're a better cocksucker than that. Show me what you got, otter."

The words should have been insulting but they only riled the otter up more, a dark stain spreading across the front of his trousers. Wrapping a paw around the base of his cock, Ronny pushed his muzzle down resolutely, ignoring how his eyes watered, and convulsed as he tickled his gag reflex. No! He had to work past it! If he could down a whole fish, he could swallow a cock again too. He could! Mewling, Ronny gulped and forced the head into his throat, angling his muzzle so that it would slide in as smoothly as was possible. The head was fat and unyielding, however, and he could only stay with his nose buried in the bull's crotch for a few moments before dragging himself back for much needed breath.

"Better..." Cormac crooned, patting the top of the otter's head. "But your time is running out. Get me off, otter, so we can get on too with our, ah, *session*."

Ronny didn't have to be told twice. Though he knew his own pleasure would go unsatisfied that day, at least in the sense of orgasm, he took greater pleasure in servicing the bull, a larger and more powerful male than him. Sucking with enough force that his cheeks hollowed in, the otter groaned and arched his back, flicking his imagination over to the notion that another male was fucking him while he blew the bull – double teaming him. In his mind's eye, an equine grabbed his hips and yanked him back, driving in past the medial ring without care for his comfort while the bull pinched his ear and shot his load down his throat. Scraping for breath, the otter gagged as the bull grabbed his muzzle and drove in just like how he imagined, the male rumbling dominantly up from the pit of his belly. He didn't play around when it came to getting off, that much was certain!

Snorting, the bull drove into the otter's muzzle, paw on the back of his head so he couldn't pull away. Ronny gagged as the bull thrust, using his muzzle like a toy as he hammered in as roughly as if he was fucking his under-tail. The otter quivered, submitting to the welcome abuse as his eyes fell lidded, world overcome by the brown bull's abdomen and a cock sliding over his tongue. Nothing else mattered in that moment and his body was entirely preoccupied with balancing on the mental brink of orgasm while he serviced his personal trainer, something far from what he had been expecting upon entering the gym that morning. The bull huffed above him, fat cock sliding slickly in as the muscles in his haunches trembled, trousers falling down to his calves without recourse. Pre-cum spurted – he'd never had that before! – with increasing intensity and frequency into his mouth and the back of his throat and he knew in a sudden flash of certainty that the bull was about to cum and cum hard.

Slamming in one last time, the bull lowed and shuddered, muscle rippling, as he unloaded in the willing muzzle. His cock jerked, sending throbbing spurts of thick seed straight down the otter's throat an instance before he was ready. Ronny trembled, holding on to Cormac as if for dear life, as he fought to swallow each jet, throat working furiously even as cum bubbled back up in his mouth. It drooled out of the corners of his lips and dripped off his muzzle, adding to the stains that would be difficult to explain away on his clothes.

The otter coughed and gulped down the last drops of cum as Cormac withdrew his softening cock from the smaller fur's muzzle with a satisfied huff of warm air. Ronny's chest heaved, regaining lost breath, as he devotedly leaned in to lap over the cock before

Cormac could pull lack even more, running his tongue around the tip to catch every drop of cum he could reach. Chuckling appreciatively, satisfied mirth rumbled up from the bull's chest and he cupped his paw around the otter's cheek, a trickle of cum staining his fur. Yes, the otter would do very well indeed. And training sessions would be even more interesting going forward, mark his words.

"Stick with me and I'll make sure you stick with the gym for a long, long time."

He smiled down at the otter cleaning up his cock with languid laps of his tongue. Ronny blushed and nodded, muscles aching in more than the expected places as he forgot where he was, drowning in bull musk and the rich taste of cum. His forearms trembled against Cormac's thighs and the bull laughed throatily, leaning back against the wall as his hoof nudged the otter's legs further apart.

"A very long time."

Don't Tell the Wife

Licking his muzzle, the red fox leaned back on the bench and raised his paws to the bar for another set – not his first of the day. The gym was packed with furs and his black lips twisted into a grunt as he brought the bar down to his chest, back flat for the time being, and thrust it upwards in a smooth line, arms trembling. Sweat darkened patches under his arms but he ignored it as he repeated the motion, the half-rack towering above him. His eyes followed the path of the bar and he lost himself in the motion, muscles working to overcome a failing in strength that could only be rectified through moving iron.

He re-racked the bar with a clang of metal on metal, sweat pouring off his forehead as fur stuck to his muzzle and head, soaked between the ears.

When he sat up again, muscles burning, he took a gulp from his supermarket water bottle, plastic crinkling in as his throat worked thirstily. The set had not exhausted him, although it was a nice burn. He could do better. But that was not his goal of the day, to reach a new high, not by a long shot. It was not that he wasn't working out, of course not. It was just that he liked doing other things at the gym too. For example, enjoying the eye candy on show.

It was a new gym to him, though that notion was nothing new. Silver, as he had come to be known despite being a red fox, had proven himself to be a dab hand at getting kicked out of gyms and health clubs, lasting no longer than a few months at each one in turn. Huffing, he added a couple of weight plates to the barbell, sliding the clamps back into place afterwards with a slight scrape of metal. Getting booted was a pain in the tail, though it could not be helped when it came down to it. After all, it was not *his* fault that he rather liked lifting his tail for other males in the sauna or the gym when it was quieter or even after hours. One of his best deals had been with a personal trainer who took him on for more intimate personal training amongst the rigs and racks when the rest of the gym patrons had left for the night.

He should see Malcolm again.

Perhaps he played into his stereotype as a fox but, hey, who could blame him when there were so many choices out there? Resting on the adjustable bench, his eyes roamed the weight room with the half and full racks lining one side and dumbbells stacked in the long rack on the other. There was more than enough equipment for everyone, though his eyes focused on a more tempting sight.

The black bull doing dumbbell pullovers on another bench caught his eye and smiled with parted lips, muscles bulging as he returned his flittering concentration to his lift. Silver smiled in return and tilted his head to the side, paw tucked into the waistband of his jogging bottoms. He had never learned the bull's name even if he knew exactly how the male's cock felt dumping a load of cum down his throat.

Wiping sweat from his brow with the little blue gym towel, the fox sprung lightly to his hind paws and pulled the weight plates from the bar to replace them neatly on the half-rack behind. It was bad form to leave weights laying around for anyone to step on or have to move before setting up for their own exercise and, despite his extracurricular activities, he left every machine or rack in pristine condition. As he stood, he flexed and stretched his arms over his head, fur pulling taut over lightly developed muscle. Silver was one for strength rather than mass and his lean, tightly packed muscle had deceived more than one suitor who had thought to pin him down with little effort at all. The fox smirked at the memory and padded across the Olympic matting to the locker rooms through which he could access the pool. His burn out bench press sets were good and done, the strength part of his workout complete.

Now for some more interesting cardio, something to better hold his attention than the treadmill.

A smile brightened across his muzzle as he walked into the changing room with metal lockers lining almost every wall, keys dangling from those still unused. It was a single room and, standing in the entranceway, the fox raked his gaze over every inch of it, taking note of which furs perched on the wooden benches in the centre with hooks for hanging up their clothes rising above. It was partly occupied by three furs, all going about their business with little care or time for the others half-naked around them. With their lack of diligence, it was a good thing Silver had more than enough looks for all of them. There were no secluded spots in which to change and that was exactly how the fox liked it.

Stalking to his locker with a cocky tilt to his muzzle, Silver dug the key out of his pocket and delved inside, searching through his rucksack for a pair of swim trunks that would be revealing enough for his sense of style. He grumbled and thrust his head into the locker, not thinking to drag the backpack out instead. Tongue sticking out of the corner of his mouth in concentration, he didn't notice the shadow of another gym goer falling across his back, blocking out the glaring overhead lighting strips.

A heavy paw landed on his right shoulder and Silver jumped, smacking the top of his skull into the locker. He cursed, fur standing on end, and backed up, rubbing his head as pain spread across the site of impact. It had not been a hard hit, and he would probably be okay, yet embarrassment seared his cheeks a burning crimson to match his fur. He could only be glad that his fur hid the majority of it, though furs with more acute senses could always tell when someone else was blushing.

Turning on his heel, the fox stared into a broad, bare chest that blocked his view of the locker room. Looking up from the dirty-red coat and black nipples standing up gloriously from the other fur's pecs, Silver caught the eye of a leering bongo, one paw back behind his head as if to show off his muscles. A pair of grey horns rose straight up from his head, at first angling outwards but then curving in as if to meet after a few inches, framed by two petal-shaped ears. The fox's eyes were drawn to the stranger's biceps, bulging massively as his chest and stomach rippled with muscle, fat cut away to reveal abdominals that Silver ached to drag his tongue over, again and again. By the gods above, he'd worship that stomach!

Well, there was no question about whether or not he wanted the bongo, at some point. Silver would do it on his terms though.

Leaning against the lockers, Silver played off his embarrassment with a light chuckle and ran his paw down the bongo's chest, muscles tensing beneath his fingertips. The very tips of the pale, cream-hued stripes that ran around the bongo's back to his sides peeked into view as the male shifted, a good head and shoulders taller than the lithe vulpine. Wrapping a familiar mental paw around his gym persona, the fox's brown eyes glimmered with wicked delight.

"Hey, cutie." Silver winked flirtatiously and wagged his tail, careful to add in a slight sway to his hips. "What can a fox do for *you* then?"

A large, black tongue snaked out to curl over the side of the mammal's muzzle, which boasted a band of lighter red-brown between a pair of dark amber eyes and a soft, grey nose. Silver shivered to think what he could do with that tongue. Sucking it between his lips or feeling it dig into his tight tail hole before the bongo moved over his body to take him with a nice, hard shaft.

The fox shook himself.

"Oh, many things..."

The bongo's lips twisted into a smirk and he leaned on the lockers, one paw with hoofed fingertips beside Silver's head. Unease stirred in the fox's chest and he curled his paws into fists, calming his breathing for the moment that instinct threatened to overwhelm him, telling him he was trapped and it was either time for flight or fight. Feral instinct was a real bitch at times. Instead of allowing panic to rear its ugly head, the fox stepped smoothly to the side and ducked under the bongo's arm, though he allowed his coat to brush the hoofer's side as he passed. He was not a complete slave to lingering instinct, after all.

"I would love to hear about them," Silver retorted smoothly from his new position beside the bongo, heart hammering in his chest. "But, for now, I'm going to pop into the pool. Would you care to join me?"

Only one answer had ever been given to that question, in his experience, and the bongo was about to subvert everything the fox had ever known.

"No."

Silver's ears twitched and uncertainty flashed across his eyes, narrowing ever so slightly at the corners. What was up with the bongo and his leering eyes?

"No? I was under the impression you wanted to talk? So, what is it?"

He blinked, confused but unwilling to let it show outwardly as he stood tall and crossed his arms over his chest in a less impressive show of muscle than what the bongo was able to put on.

Exhaling heavily, the bongo blew sour breath into the fox's face, laced with the acrid aroma of cigarette smoke. Coughing hard enough to make his eyes water, Silver waved his paw in front of his muzzle and took another step back away from his still open locker. The other furs in the room, an antelope and a wolf, were quiet, watching the action with avid eyes.

When the bongo did not speak, Silver rolled his eyes and made as if to walk away, to turn his back on the silly fur, but was stopped by a paw gripping his bicep far, far too tightly for comfort. Eyes darkening, the bongo leaned in, dragging the fox closer at the same time. Silver's breath caught in his throat and he tried to pull away, only to find his strength inadequate in the face of the larger male. In the corner of his eye, he saw the wolf stand, tail still in unspoken threat.

"I'm past talking to you, slut."

The bongo rolled his eyes, using the derogatory term as casually as if he was talking to a close friend of many years in candid conversation.

"I know all I need to know about you and more than I'd like to know. You're going to have my dick in your mouth in the next two minutes, runt."

Though his heart leapt into his throat, Silver stifled the surge of anger and twisted suddenly, yanking his arm from the bongo's grasp with the element of surprise. Growling, the male lunged for him but the fox danced out of reach, tail tucked down over his rump as his eyes narrowed. Something in his chest tightened, flaring up into heat that seeped through his veins. Who the fuck did the bongo bastard think he was to demand sex from him? A fucking blowjob? Like he just did everything on fucking cue! And he wasn't a slut! Who gave a damn if he had fun with others or not? He wasn't at their god damn disposal.

With space between him and the bongo, Silver fell back on his natural boldness, hind paw tapping the cream-flecked floor as he bit down his anger. Not about to get thrown out of another gym for a reason deemed less than good enough, he turned away, leaving his locker open as he thought to fetch someone with a little more authority at the gym. The front desk was always manned and, at such a strength and training focused establishment, he couldn't see them tolerating the abuse. The irony of him breaking the rules with frequent disregard was not lost on him, however, and the fox grimaced.

"Sorry, *darling*," Silver said over his shoulder with a dismissive flick of his paw. "Not if you're going to bully me around like that. Try again later. Or try talking to a lad first, hey?"

"You're going to get in that room and suck my cock right now," the bongo hissed into his muzzle, hot breath washing over Silver's snout. "Or else."

Swallowing hard, Silver refused to quail and stood nose to nose with the bongo, eyes flaring fiercely. Just because he liked to have his fun with others didn't mean he could be forced into anything? That was a different fucking matter entirely!

He straightened, setting his shoulders back. He had enough witnesses to back him up. If the bongo towed him away, one of the others would step in or grab one of the members of gym staff to aid him. Not that he couldn't take care of himself.

"Get in there now...or else what?" He challenged, lips tugging up. "What, exactly, do you think you're going to do here? You ain't got nothing. Drag me in? Someone will see. I'm sure that will go down fucking well, hey?"

The bongo's eyes narrowed as the wolf looking between them chuckled, seeing the folly in the ploy that the bully demanded. Leaning in close to the fox, he put them nose to nose, snorting warm air over the fox's muzzle. Silver grimaced but held his ground as the bongo's lips tightened into a cruel, thin line.

"Or I'll tell your wife what you've been doing during your gym time..." He said too quietly for the others in the locker room to hear, his tone low. "If you can even call it that, cock sucker."

Silver froze, fur flattening to his body. Blinking, his vision flickered with grey and the room seemed to tilt around him sickeningly, making him sway as if he had enjoyed far too much to drink one evening. His lungs tightened and he struggled to breathe, tail tucked down over his buttocks as if for some semblance of protection. But there was no protection to be had from the cold, hard truth.

He had a wife. A wife that he never spoke about once he was within the walls of the health club, gymnasium or anything other of that persuasion. She was beautiful. But she wasn't a muscled stud. She didn't have the hold over him that these males did. It would break her to know.

She could never know. Never, ever, ever. The fox closed his eyes, pulling scattered nerves back together through ragged willpower.

Silver swallowed, ears slanting back to his skull. He was well and truly had, done for. He didn't want to even consider what his wife would do to him if she found out. Or how she would feel. Oh, he'd never meant to hurt her. It was just...sex and love were different for him, very different. He liked both sexes. What else was a fox to do? He could not justify it.

With a sick roll of nausea in the pit of his stomach, there was only one option. If only his tail did not quiver at the thought of another cock in his muzzle, regardless of the conditions it was under. Yet he wanted it and that notion was at his core still, yearning to take that dominance of the bongo's and reward it with submission.

The bongo had him and, damn…it was hot. It shouldn't have been and yet that didn't change anything, no, not in the slightest, not as heat rushed to his crotch. Silver's cock thickened slightly, plumping up needily in anticipation of what was to come.

Knowing that he had nailed the fox's weak spot, the bongo stood back and flicked his ropey tail, thwacking it into his thigh. He did not need to use brute force as he stepped away, eyes smug and head tilted cockily. The fox would follow, already broken to his fate.

"Come with me, fox."

Head lowered, Silver tried to paint a smile on his muzzle and stood beside the bongo, his white tail tip twitching anxiously. He couldn't stay still, shifting on the balls of his paws to adjust his weight, senses rampant on high alert. His cock swelled in his jogging bottoms to bulge out subtly and Silver resisted the urge to cover it with his paws, for that would only draw more attention to his shame. His cheeks flushed with heat and he ran his tongue around the inside of his suddenly very dry mouth, avoiding the bongo's gaze as he waited for him to make the next move. The fox, after all, had no more reasonable moves in his assnal left to make. His side of the play was over.

"Is there a problem here?"

They looked to the side, one with confidence and one with fear, to see the grey-furred wolf standing there in casual gym wear and a concerned look in his eye. Gulping, Silver shook his head, blood roaring in his ears.

"N-no," he stammered. "Nothing's wrong at all, t-thank you. Just a joke. Friend caught me a bit unawares and it's after gym time, you know. Not really with it today."

He slipped more easily into the lie as he spoke, hating how easily it slipped from his lips. He was well used to lying but this lie left a sour taste in his mouth that no amount of lapping his lips could dissipate.

Satisfied by the albeit stammering explanation, the wolf nodded and backed off, returning his attention to his belongings and changing out of his sweaty gym clothes. He kept a careful eye on the bongo and fox, however, the light flick of his tail betraying his watchfulness. Huffing with a dramatic roll of his eyes that was entirely unnecessary, the bongo jerked his head, smiling a smile that did not warm the light in his eyes.

"Come on, fox, let's go check out the pool," the bongo murmured loudly enough for show as he clapped a far from friendly paw down on Silver's shoulder.

He strove not to shudder away and instead bobbed his muzzle, taking the lead as if he was going to show the bongo where the pool was, assuming that the male was yet to explore it for himself. Padding lightly over the flooring in his gym trainers, the fox swallowed his nerves, snakes writhing in his belly, and rounded the corner out of the locker room. Silver forgot about the open locker door swinging open behind him but no one else thought to mention it, least of all the bongo with a cocky saunter to his stride.

He entered the corridor leading to the pool, nose twitching at the overpowering scent of chlorine. Some establishments used gentler chemicals and covered up scents so that it did not strain sensitive noses; this gym was not one of them. Any fur wishing to complain could do so and end the day regardless with the stench of chemicals running coassly through his or her fur.

Silver's mind was not on the obnoxious stink, however, and he felt the presence of the bongo all too acutely as he paused at the door to the supply cupboard, paw trembling. He did not want to go in.

Yet he had no choice. His hind paws moved for him, lust dictating all he had to do, though, perhaps that time, he'd just needed an excuse. With a lump in his throat, the fox ducked into the cupboard quickly, afraid someone would see, and let the door swing back in the bongo's face. Let him open it himself. The fox would not make it easy for him. His heart pounded against his ribcage as he backed into the dark room, paw bumping a mop bucket situated beside a stack of weight plates. There really was everything and anything in a gym supply room. He would have found it funnier another time.

The bongo stepped inside with a grin more suited to a predator as he groped his bulge, which pushed more obviously against the front of his gym trousers, demanding release. And, if release was not readily given, Silver had no doubt in his mind that the bongo would take it by force. That's where his threats came into play, curling into corners of the fox's mind that he never wanted to explore ever again.

As the bongo followed him to the back of the small room, the fox shrank away, lips curling up from his teeth. He hated being cornered. Silver still did not even know the bongo's name. Though that in itself was not unusual for him.

The bongo leaned on the wall, paws either side of the fox's head, and grinned toothily. One tooth was crooked and Silver latched on to this imperfection to lend himself courage, trying to ignore the male's rancid breath.

"What the fuck are you talking about my wife for?" He hissed through gritted teeth, talking the big talk while his knees shook. "You have no fucking business bringing her up. Do you know Sylvia?"

The bongo tilted his head, eyes cunningly sharp in the dim light.

"Oh, I know Sylvia very well, my slutty vulpine."

The bongo stroked his muzzle with a rough caress, dragging the back of his paw back along Silver's face when the fox shuddered away from his touch.

"And you would do well to remember that," he told him. "I could destroy your life, your little world, in a single message. Do you think Sylvia would like to know?"

Silver refused to think about it, turning his muzzle to the side and out of the bongo's rough paw. He couldn't help but realise that, even though they were well out of sight of anyone else, the bongo had not yet made a sexual move on him. The most he had done so far was intimidate him and successfully so. Thinking quickly, the fox's mind raced. Perhaps the bongo was not as tough as he would have the fox believe. Silver nipped the inside of his lip and took a deep breath.

"I won't do it." He folded his arms across his chest. "You're all fucking talk, you are. Ain't going to –"

The bongo snarled, a deep, guttural sound that sent tremors through Silver's gut and made him push away, pinning himself to the wall. A predator should have made that sound. Not to be toyed with, the bongo's paw lashed out and struck Silver's throat, hurling him to the side with a strangled yelp lost with his breath. The bongo followed as he fell, reaching out for the fox with a manic gleam to his eye, a fur that had lost his senses entirely.

"Either you get down on your knees and suck my dick right now," the bongo whispered, paw closing around Silver's throat, "or I tell your wife exactly what you are doing during your *gym time*. You don't fucking need me to repeat it, do you, cunt?"

The fox shook his head, kicking out and striking nothing as he whined against the bongo's hold, his body a traitor to his better senses. Why did his cock have to bulge out so? Why, why, why, why, why? He scratched at the bongo's arms and wheezed, chest heaving as he gasped at non-existent air.

"Please..." Silver whimpered breathlessly even as his cock grew hard and throbbing in his trousers, the lack of underwear allowing blood to rush unrestricted to his member. "Don't tell her. She doesn't have to know. She's happier *not* knowing!"

"Then why do you do it, slut?" He demanded, paw tightening to cut off the fox's air supply as he dragged him upward, hind paws dangling. "Tell me, why? Why do you go around raising your tail for everyone?"

The hind paws of the vulpine kicked in the air and he scrabbled at the bongo, eyes bulging out of their sockets as his vision flickered, misting over with grey. Snorting, the bongo dropped him and the fox crashed to the ground, rolling on to his back as he wheezed and rubbed his throat, eyes on the mammal's hooves as they brushed his fur too lightly.

"Huh. Figures. No fucking answer a slut like you can give."

Gasping, the fox's lungs heaved and he ducked his head as his tongue lolled from his muzzle while he recovered on all fours. The tip of his brush dipped to the floor and his ears followed suit, regardless of his cock ached and ached. If his cock wasn't harder than ever, he would have sunk his fist into the bongo's stomach. As it was, the red rod of vulpine flesh drooled with pre-cum, clear fluid beading on the head and begging to be lapped up. Silver gulped and stifled the urge to roll his hips forward as a thick, fleshy pole of bongo meat sprung into his face, released from the confines of the larger male's workout trousers. He was not the one who was going to be receiving a blowjob.

"Suck it."

Flinching, Silver bobbed his muzzle and leaned in, parting his lips to engulf that throbbing, pink length in his mouth. Not the largest he had taken, it still strained his lips into a wide O-shape and he brought his paws up to the male's thighs, curling his fingers into the muscle to anchor himself in the moment. His tongue pressed to the underside of the length and he slid down until the tip nuzzled the back of his throat, letting him know that he could go no further. Drops of moisture trickled down his throat and, instinctively, Silver gulped, drinking down the bongo's pre-cum as if it was the finest wine in the world.

The fox should have been revolted, he should have pulled away in disgust, sworn at the bongo for making him perform such an act when he was in no way, shape or form into the act. At least, that was what Silver told himself, preferring his own lie to what his body sang for. Yet he made no move to pull away and thoughts of his wife were far from the forefront of his mind. If only it didn't taste so good. Silver whined, the sound muffled by the length. Why did it have to taste so good?

Groaning, the bongo huffed and rolled his hips out, lazily fucking the fox's muzzle as he casually rested a dominant paw on his head. The hoofed fingertips scratched through his head fur and the fox shuddered, though not from any urge to pull away. Instead, his legs buckled so he sat back on his heels, trainers digging into his rump, and freed the bongo's balls from the confines of his jogging bottoms with a quick swipe of his paw, so swift that he had the pair of orbs cradled before the controlling male could even blink. Raising an eyebrow, he huffed above the fox and pinched an ear between a thumb and forefinger to spark a sharp twinge of pain. Just to remind the fox who really was in charge, regardless of whose balls Silver cupped oh so reverently.

Silver rolled the bongo's balls between his fingers as he allowed the male to rock into his muzzle, holding his muzzle obediently still for the throbbing length. The hoofer grunted, a deep, guttural sound than made lesser males drop their ears, and drove in deep, eking out a little more depth with every thrust as if to tease the fox with his masculine power. Submission shivered in a cool trickle down his spine and the fox yipped quietly for breath when the bongo pulled back, dragging in quick gulps of air whenever he was permitted. The soreness around his throat served as an acute reminder of how his breath had been cut short and he almost wished for it again. Maybe if he asked the bongo nicely...

The fox flinched. He shouldn't think like that! He had to remember that he wasn't doing any of this on his own terms. It wasn't like all the other times with the males he willingly served on his knees. They were different, very different.

And the bongo was in control, well and truly. He could not possibly forget that or pretend otherwise, half gagging on the male's shaft as it teased into his throat, threatening to go deeper. Anxious, Silver tried to subtly pull his head back enough so that he could control the depth but his new friend wasn't having any of that, oh no. The bongo smirked down at him and shoved the back of the fox's head so that his nose pressed to his crotch and Silver convulsed with suppressed coughs, fighting down his gag reflex with every ounce of control he boasted. A smaller part of him thrummed with pride that he was able to take every inch, though his eyes watered terribly.

"This is all you're really good for, isn't it, slut?" He chuckled, driving in to the hilt with a lusty, full throated moan. "Taking a cock deep in your muzzle."

The bongo patted his head mockingly, treating him like a feral dog to be trained as he pleased. Using the full length of Silver's muzzle and throat, the bongo growled dominantly, the sound rolling through the supply cupboard, and thrust brutally, jamming the head right down the fox's throat. Silver hacked a cough and submitted to the abuse, eyes watering through a haze of lust as his cock throbbed and spurted pre-cum down his throat, the salty treat bypassing his tongue as the bongo huffed.

He thrust roughly, uncaring for the fox's comfort, as Silver released his balls, letting them slap into his white furred chin as he whined and gulped, throat tightening sporadically around the fat cock. The bongo's crotch whacked his nose with every thrust and he trembled, utterly helpless with his tail tucked between his legs and pre-cum soaking shamefully through his trousers. He could have knelt there in that moment forever, if the bongo had been so inclined to use him, and quite happily so. Even the most virile male, however, would reach climax sooner or later. And the bongo was aware of movement on the other side of the door even if his slutty little fox was not, furs passing their refuge along on their way. Sooner or later, someone would investigate.

The fox's eyes grew wider and wider as the bongo's thrusts became urgent, bordering on desperate as he neared the point of no return. And he had no intention of pulling out – the fox would have to take every inch and every drop that the male had to give, if he wanted his wife to remain blissfully oblivious to his activities. Then he could spend all the time on his knees he wanted. Slamming in a final time, the bongo gave a load groan as he ejaculated, resting his cock in the fox's throat to pour cum straight down. Silver had no choice but to gulp quickly to keep the spurts coming, stimulating the bongo's cock until he drained every drop of seed from his balls, which were as full and plump as ever.

Silver bet that the bongo stud had even more to give even as his cock quickly softened in the fox's muzzle, slipping out with a lewd drizzle of cum and saliva. He couldn't be certain that he could take another round, however, and looked down at the bongo's cloven hooves, spread apart for balance, and how the fabric of his clothing draped beautifully over his muscle. In any other circumstance, he would have loved to feel those muscles moving over him and a part of him still craved it, the throb of male flesh in his paw.

Wiping his cock off on Silver's muzzle, the bongo grinned and turned his attention to the fox's taut rump, muscled from years of gym work that was not entirely in the squat rack. He dragged the weak-limbed fox up by the scruff of the neck and, ignoring noise on the other side of the door, pushed him into the racking, muzzle thrust down. Staring at bottles of floor cleaner and clothes piled high, Silver bit his lip as his jogging bottoms were yanked down around his ankles, baring his backside and cock jutting out proudly from his crotch like a flag pole. It was smaller than the bongo's and the male wasted no time in chuckling, wrapping a paw around it and pressing his hips to the vulpine's rump possessively.

He leaned forward and hissed in the fox's ear as the door opened a crack, the murmur of voices growing louder. The tapered tip of the bongo's cock kissed his tail hole, cum his only trace of lube, and tightened his grip on his partner for the session, words curling on sinuous trails through the fox's mind. Silver's eyes grew wide.

"Maybe I will tell your wife after all..."

But that would be the lie Silver needed to tell himself, again and again, just to keep him coming back to feed the bongo's lust…and his own.

His wife would not know. But the fox, one way or another, would get all of his needs met.

Squats

The call of metal on metal rang through the gym as the late evening crowd worked muscles until they tore, only to be rebuilt stronger and larger than before, ever becoming more and more powerful. Though small, the gym hosted a dedicated clientele of bodybuilders and power lifters, amongst those simply trying to maintain a healthy lifestyle with plenty of iron in their diet. To the most hardened of lifters, the gym floor could not be denied its blood and sweat, grunts and groans reverberating in an air to rival sins committed within bedroom walls. Muscle fibres repairing themselves over the next few days would drive them towards their goals, whether that was strength, size or something else entirely, and it was that constant progress that kept many a gym-goer addicted to their sport of choice.

A pair often seen together worked in the power cage, a full rack with four vertical beams, bolted into the ground as if to cage the trainee inside. The ruffled wolf, Si, stood with his knees patiently locked and a laden barbell across the back of his shoulders. Bare of shirt, his grey fur stuck to his skin beneath the unflattering light, his shorts reaching the midpoint of his thighs. There was little need to wear more clothing than that in their kind of gym, only getting in the way of lifts when fur was usually enough protection for their anthro kind. The wolf's paws steadied the bar as his training partner, a larger, heftier brown bear, stood at his back, paws a few inches from the barbell to act as his spotter. It was not the easiest of tasks to spot another fur during squats but some found it motivational, so to speak, particularly if the correct form thrust their rumps back against their spotter's crotch.

But that pleasure was only for a certain kind of males to enjoy.

Mike's brow furrowed as he dropped slowly, following the wolf's motion as the lupine sank into a clean squat, muscles throbbing with the strain of the weight. Grinding his teeth together, Si's knees nipped in for the briefest of moments at the bottom of the lift and the bear growled warningly. Si flicked his ears. One warning to hold his form did the trick and, with a grunt, he rose out of the squat, completing the eighth and final repetition of his set.

He stepped forward and set the bar down on the hooks, groaning as the line of pressure across his shoulders was abruptly removed. A line ran horizontally through his fur where the bar had compressed it and the bear rubbed his thumbs over the imprint soothingly, leaning in closer than would have been comfortable for average training partners. Tail wagging, the wolf arched and pushed his shoulders back into Mike's touch, his sharp blue eyes half-lidded with pleasure and endorphins, nausea licking at the pit of his stomach.

They could not deny each other their little addictions, as illicit as the pleasure may have been.

The wolf rolled his shoulders and straightened, working out the kinks as a couple of other gym patrons made use of the half-racks on either side of them for bench and overhead presses respectively, adding to the gym clamour. Sometimes they could not even hear music clearly through headphones over the sound of furs working out. It didn't matter so much when they worked out together though.

"What's next on your routine?" Si panted, sweat trickling down his brow. "Don't want to slow down. Change the plates? What?"

The bear rolled his eyes and nudged Si out of the rack with his shoulder, easing him past the safety pins, designed to catch the barbell if a lift failed. He wore more than the wolf, a simple black T-shirt and pair of grey jogging bottoms, though both kept their hind paws bare for greater stability and proper lifting form. Rubbing his muzzle, he smirked without a word as he removed the coloured weight plates from each end of the barbell, clamps clattering to the matted floor until they were needed again.

Fiddling with his paws, the wolf resisted the urge to fold his arms across his chest like a petulant cub or sulking girlfriend.

"Mike!" The wolf growled, tail tucked down to his buttocks. "Are you even listening to me? Mike? Mike?"

In his own sweet time, Mike faced him, brown eyes wide and innocent. His black nose quivered as if he was trying to hold back laughter and he held up his paws innocently, palms facing out towards the wolf.

"Always in a hurry, you wolves," he quipped, replacing the removed plates with ones of his choosing, suited to his set style. "You'd think you lot would slow down once in a while, take it easier. Break between sets to let yourself recover. Quit the howls. It's the same for both of us here, you know, Si."

Si grinned and wagged his tail, rubbing the sweat from his bare chest with the aid of his gym towel, smelling decidedly ripe. The wolf wrinkled his muzzle, smile vanishing. He would have to remember to wash it when he was home but somehow the task always seemed to slip by him. Laundry never seemed that important even when the pile swelled into an alternate, devouring life form. It was one of his many failings and one that Mike ribbed him the most for, though only when he managed to spot it. Wolves were *excellent* at covering their tracks.

Eyeing the barbell, Simon – Si for short – took note of how much weight the bear was loading on to the bar, a great deal more than he was able to squat for ten or even eight repetitions. He sniffed, widening his eyes.

"Are you sure you can do that?" He asked, doubt ringing through his tone. "Looks like rather a lot. I know you're bigger and all but you didn't hit that PR last time. Don't push it too hard, a bit more every time, hey."

The brown bear scoffed and waved his paw dismissively, brushing excess chalk from his paws over the larger curve of his stomach. Despite being a frequent sight in the gym, Mike boasted a lifter's gut with masculine pride: a badge of honour.

"Just because you're going for shape and looks doesn't mean those with strength to share should lift lighter," he said. "What were you using today? One hundred kilos?"

Si's lips pressed together in a thin, tight line, ears slipping towards his skull but not quite touching fur.

"More than that." He refused to reveal specific numbers. "Does it matter? You don't have the quads I do."

Demonstrating his physique, he faced his friend head on, tensing his legs so that the muscle plumped out proudly, rigid with a fine, melting layer of fat over the top. Muscle on the front of the thigh was more difficult to build, but Si had worked on it over several years and had every reason to be proud of his physique. Besides his thighs and calves, his six pack was not of the alcoholic variety and his arms rippled with muscle, back tapering down to a perfect, masculine V.

Licking his black lips, Mike scratched the back of his neck and enjoyed the show.

"Nope, can't say that I do have your thighs after all," he grinned. "Maybe in bed but, nope, you got me there."

Si huffed and angled his muzzle away, though the blush beneath his fur could not be hidden from one who knew him so well.

"Perv."

"Aw, darling."

The bear held a paw to his forehead as if mortally offended, his eyes wide and suddenly girlish in their gleam.

"It's almost as if it's a *bad* thing you think I'm a pervert."

Studying Si, Mike rocked back on his heels, eyes flicking between the loaded barbell and the wolf. He licked his lips and bobbed his muzzle, seeming to come to a decision at the very moment the wolf moved towards the rack of weight plates, ready to continue with only a grumble and swish of his thickly furred tail.

"You done yet?"

"What?" Si shook his head. "Not by half. Why?"

"Cause I think we're done here," Mike retorted, peering down his snout at Si as the wolf squatted to collect a stray fifteen kilo plate.

Freezing at that tone, the wolf's ears drooped submissively to either side of his head, though he ground his teeth and fought through sheer force of will to keep them pricked. The bear had too much of an idea already of the effect he had on him, if what they had done in the bedroom the previous night was not evidence enough. Shivering, smoothed down the fur on his chest and tried not to feel the ache under his tail, sore even after the daily grind of the work day. He tried not to remember hot breath on his neck and the pleasure-pain of the bear's teeth sinking deep into his shoulder in a mating bite. Where the cuts would heal, the wolf bore the marks beneath his fur, telling scars never truly fading.

He sighed and looked away, the very tip of his tail wagging, the grey slashed through with black hairs. There was never much point in forgetting, not with Mike around to remind him.

As if knowing exactly what the wolf was thinking better than he knew himself, the bear's lips twitched in a smirk and he jerked his muzzle up and back, gesturing over his shoulder. The bulge in his jogging bottoms, easy enough to avert the eye from thus far, swelled, cock pushing out of its sheath into the fabric. Gulping, Si could not drag his eyes away, hypnotised by how that fat bulge tented out the cotton fabric obscenely, invitingly. The bear chuckled throatily. Catching the wolf's eye with some difficulty, Mike trailed his fingers suggestively over the bulge and Si's throat worked, recalling how quickly he had had to swallow that first time together to gulp down every drop of cum the bear dumped into his muzzle. Even now his throat burned for it. The salty, heady taste was an addiction in itself.

Si had many addictions. All involved Mike.

Mike chuckled, lips parting in the exhalation of breath. He looked back at Si over his shoulder, eyelids half-lowering with barely concealed desire, though the look was far from flirtatious, instead emanating raw desire. What reason did he have to pretend he was a bigger bear than he was when such a willing pup was practically whimpering at his paws? He had the wolf wrapped around his little finger and, by god, did he know it!

"Shut up and meet me in the showers, if you have nothing better to do, stud-wolf."

Si raised an eyebrow, blood roaring in his ears. Could the bear be any more obvious? In the showers? Like that would happen. But Mike called his bluff, walking across the matted room in the general direction of the showers, paws lighter than they should have been after a workout.

As the bear walked away, Si stood rooted in place, the tail of his tail flicking from side to side, lust battling with sensibilities he longed to forget.

"Thought you had some work left to do here?"

The wolf grasped at straws that he did not truly want to clutch, to draw himself away from the bear's mental hold. Oh, how much easier it would be to fold to his knees and look up at his dom, let the bear have his way with him. But in public? The thought made his heart thud as much as his legs trembled, buckling at the knees. He whined.

"All work and no play leads to a very dull day," the bear recited solemnly, stubby tail twitching in the only outward indication of his excitement. "Follow me, wolf."

"And what about other people in the gym, hm?" Si asked, ears flicking back and forward again as if to catch each and every little sound in the echoing rooms. "What if they see? What if they catch us? Where are we going?"

Mike shrugged, massive shoulders rolling nonchalantly.

"You best put on a good show for them then, if anyone's left around, pup."

Mike could not even feel bad for skipping out on a portion of his workout, trotting through the gym with a whistle on his lips. He would catch up on the weekend and, hey, it was not as if he had not gone to the gym anyway. He grinned as he paused by the lockers, dragging his towel and spare clothes from the metal container, chilled from their stay. He was just going to complete his workout with a very different activity.

The shower cubicles were private, designed to fit one fur at a time, and Mike stepped on to the cool tiles with a sigh of relief, kicking off his shoes before entering the cubicle itself. He pushed the door closed behind him without locking it and stripped off his jogging bottoms and T-shirt, slinging them back over the top of the door. They would become damp in such close proximity to the shower but he did not care to pop back outside to stow them more safely in his bag. He turned on the shower and doused himself in hot water, flattening his brown fur to his skin in abject bliss.

Mike turned his muzzle up into the stream and sighed, lifting his paws to his face to rub his muzzle clean of sweat. Despite the shorter workout of the day – hardly anything at all by his high standards – he still ached from the week at his back, every inch of him aching deep in the muscle. A day off would do him good, he could catch up on Sunday. The bear smirked. With Si.

Another fur entered the shower room behind him and the bear gave a lopsided smile. The wolf pressed his back to the inside of the shower door with his ears splayed and cheeks flushed with heat. He tilted his muzzle up defiantly, rump squashed to the door as if he was afraid of getting too close to the bear, keeping his distance as much as he was able in the confines of the cubicle. He looked from side to side, assessing the space of their private suite as spray from the shower dampened his clothes. Belatedly, he wished he had taken them off. He had an inkling, however, that he would not be even half dressed for much longer.

"Hey."

The bear's gaze smouldered.

"Hey," Si muttered in return, averting his eyes. "Hey...

Mike rumbled and faced the wolf square on, challenging him with the bulk of his body, muscle as dominant as fat. It was the difference between power lifters and body builders that was difficult to deny in the bare fur. His belly swelled with a muscle gut and, below the bulge, his fleshy-pink cock eased from its tucked in sheath, pushing from the fold of darker skin and fur into view. Arrogant in its display, Mike dipped his muzzle towards the needy length with a casual twitch, needing to give his wolf no more direction.

"Well, what are you waiting for?"

The wolf tilted his head to the side like a pup. Mike nearly laughed aloud, though held back his mirth just in time. It would not do to laugh, not when he wanted something from his friend with more than one benefit. Wouldn't want to scare off the wolf now, would he?

"Huh?"

The bear raised his paw, eyes narrowing in an easy tell.

"Get on your knees, pup."

Grasping the fur on the back of Si's head, Mike shoved him to his knees, smirking as the wolf's knees connected with the hard tiles. Though he winced, Si voiced no complaint and ducked his muzzle shyly, tail lifting in a wag over his rump. The bear dragged his muzzle n to his cock, rubbing the length of the wolf's narrower snout over his shaft. Shivering, Si whined and closed his eyes, enjoying the feel of smooth, slick skin against his fur. Unconsciously, he licked his lips, wanting it deep in his muzzle after only the slightest bit of provocation.

Si whimpered and looked up at the bear towering over him, forgetting the throb of pain in his knees as the bear glowered, fingers tightening in his scruff.

He did not have to ask what the bear wanted and parted his lips willingly. He knew Mike all too well, though every time together still made his heart thud as if it was the very first time all over again. Clenching his tail hole in memory that could not be quashed, he dove down on Mike's cock, taking it deep into his muzzle. The tip jammed into the back of his throat and the wolf jerked, paws flying up to the bear's legs as he squeezed and closed his eyes, fighting down his gag reflex. The bear rubbed between the wolf's ears. Si was always a bit over ambitious when it came to cock sucking.

It was a good trait for a slut to have.

Murring around the bear's shaft, Si bobbed his muzzle slowly, luxuriating in the taste and sensation. Rising and falling on the smooth cock, his rump swayed, imagining how good it would feel deep inside him, pushing past his anal ring. He pressed his tongue to its underside, lips pursed into a tight O and sucked hard, spurred on by the little thrusts of his hips the bear gave in return. He was strict in self-restraint, enjoying pleasure where it was demanded, though it had become clear throughout the course of their liaisons that the bear's body gave away more than his words ever would.

Gripping Mike's leg in an iron-clasp, the wolf whimpered around the fat length stretching his lips wide in a familiar strain. Oh, it had been too long since they had last had a moment together. Maybe friends with benefits would have to be something more, one day, but for now this was all they could have. It was better than nothing and the wolf forced his muzzle down far so that his nose pressed into Mike's damp crotch fur, the thicker tufts tickling his nose.

The bear grunted and shoved Mike's head back against the cubicle door, pinning it shut as he trapped Si in place with his bulk. Hips bucking, the bear snarled under his breath as his lips curled up from his teeth, and humped the wolf's muzzle savagely. The long, deep strokes made Si tremble and he reached between the bear's legs to rub and adore his heavy balls with the gentlest of touches as he submitted, allowing Mike to use his muzzle exactly as he willed. He was but a toy in the larger, stronger bear's paws. What was a physique when he could be subdued under a stronger paw? His skull pressed to the cold door and he whimpered as the bear thrust and pushed down on his head, demanding a deeper thrust for each, ruthless, driving roll of his hips.

Perfect form, of course, was a requisite to all.

Mike's chest heaved, fighting for breath the blasted wolf stole from him in his weakest of moments, legs shaking from the strain of thrusting in such a confined space. Leaning over the lupine, he arched his back unnaturally and furrowed his brow, tiring of the blowjob, as delicious as the wolf's hot muzzle could be. No, this evening he wanted something more, something much more. More than a workout and quick fuck in the showers. A simple lick and suck would not do for him this time.

"Up, pup."

Si jumped to his paws, fully submissive, and wagged his tail in as appeasing a manner as he could manage, the force of it tugging the fabric back and forth across his rump. His soaked-through jogging bottoms clung to his legs, but he did not care one bit. Neither did Mike. The problem of leaving the gym in wet clothes, however, would be a problem to be addressed at a later time. They had each other to consider in the moment.

Spinning the wolf around to face the wall adjacent to another cubicle, Mike yanked down the wolf's trousers, baring his rump as Si's tapered canine cock sprung free in a judder of flesh. The muscled curves of the wolf's ass made him murr in delight, running an appreciative paw over the hard tone.

"It's all those *squats*, bitch..."

Panting, Si pressed his cheek to the door and wagged his tail weakly, grunting as it was yanked up by a coass paw. Mike ran the tips of his claws through Si's tail fur and smirked as the wolf shivered, his body a toy at the bear's whim. Holding the wolf to the wall with one, strong paw, Mike grunted and ground his cock between Si's rump cheeks, letting the water and soaked fur ease his path. The tip dragged over the wolf's tail hole and he trembled, tail flipped up obediently as the bear brought his fingers to his muzzle, moistening them with his own saliva, though there would not be much lubrication to ease his entry.

The wolf squirmed and peered back over his shoulder, blinking rapidly against the spray from the shower as he craned to see what the bear was doing, anticipating a swift entry. Further away, somewhere in the weights room, a hefty weight plate dropped to the floor with a thud. Though Si's ears flicked to the side to catch the sound, he would not have done anything even if another fur was pacing back and forth on the other side of the shower door waiting for them to be good and done and out of there.

When no touch or gentle lube – shampoo? – was forthcoming, he ground his teeth together and whined.

"Aren't you gonna..." He started, a blush seeping across his cheeks.

The wolf left the question open ended. To his dismay, Mike merely shook his head and pushed a finger deep into the pup's tail hole. Si arched his back, clenching his jaw together until the joint ached fiercely, anxious hurt distracting him from the sudden penetration. In a mixture of pleasure and pain, the wolf pushed back on to the digit thrusting into him and moaned breathily as a second was added, curling up against his prostate. It was difficult to be incompliant for long with Mike. The bear would take what he wanted anyway.

"Nope."

Ignoring Si's eyes widening, the bear pulled back his fingers and replaced them with the tip of his cock, slick with water. The wolf bit his lip hard, blood beading and bleeding into the water as he struggled to take Mike, relaxing the best he could as his poor tail hole automatically tried to deny entrance to the intruder, clenching tightly. But the bear was not to be denied, even if he could be considerate towards his partner. He would not want to break his pup. His size and bulk aided his smooth thrust in, bearing down, and Mike gently guided his cock deeper until his crotch nestled in against the wolf's muscled rump. With the curve of his stomach resting above Si's tail, he growled deep in his throat and clamped one paw down on top of Si's, as if he needed further confirmation as to who was in charge.

"Oh..." Si moaned, lips parted and muzzle turned up. "You... You feel so much – ah – thicker without lube."

"Oh, really now?" Mike panted, muzzle next to the wolf's as he slowly thrust. "Maybe we'll have to go without a little more often then, won't we?"

Si shuddered.

"Without?"

"Mhm."

Mike rolled his hips slowly and sensually, power thrumming through every stroke into Si's rump. He did not need to exert much strength to keep the wolf in place with a paw between his shoulder blades and relished in his own power, taking the wolf's hot, tight hole at the pace that pleased him. Where was the sense in rushing when he had all the time in the world to enjoy his little pup?

Growling, Mike drove in his full length, crotch flush with Si's backside. The wolf groaned deep in the back of his throat.

"You'll *break* me."

Si whimpered, caught up in imagining further fucking without the assistance of the ever-present tube of lubricant, usually an essential for any anal play. Mike laughed, chest rumbling, and shoved in deep in a series of rough thrusts in which he barely pulled back a couple of inches before rocking forward again with a snarl.

"Then I'll use your muzzle, slut puppy."

Groaning, the wolf submitted to his alpha, ducking his muzzle down against the door. Soreness emanated from his tail hole and he panted through an open muzzle as ecstasy toyed with its edge, tail twitching back and forth in restless arousal. Every thrust ground deliciously over his prostate and he slammed his paw into the door, the pain in his fist a distraction as sensation threatened to overwhelm him. His cock drooled pre-cum in a steady trickle, concealed only by the steady stream of water. The wolf moaned. It was too much, far too much!

Si's cock throbbed in a sudden flare of sensation, suddenly warm in the grasp of a paw larger than his. The bear chuckled throatily into his ear as he stroked, pumping Si's needy shaft in time with his thrusts. Slowly but surely, Mike's pace increased and his thrusts came with greater urgency, animalistic desire driving him towards a peak his body demanded.

"Don't cum yet, puppy," the bear growled. "Wait for me."

"Yes..."

"Yes, what?"

Si licked his lips.

"Yes, sir."

Pulling back away from the door, Mike spun Si to face the rear wall of the cubicle, shoving the wolf beneath the hot stream of water and down into a squat. The wolf yelped but obediently allowed himself to be handled as easily as a puppy in its master's paws, spreading his legs wide and staying up on his toes to give Mike the space he needed to thrust. With one paw on the wolf's shoulder, Mike grunted as he drove into Si's tight backside, ignoring the yips of pain as he forced the wolf down on his cock, tail hole straining whether he liked it or not. The pup had to like it. He always came back for more.

Mike squeezed his paw around the wolf's dick, the shower washing away needy pre-cum as quickly as Si could produce it. He planted his hind paws firmly on the roughed-up floor – for grip when slippery, he could only assume – and thrust like a demon, using his leverage on Si's shoulder to hold the wolf's body as still as possible, subjecting him to the entirety of each and every thrust. Si gave a high-pitched whine as the paw on his cock stroked more urgently, forced to the peak of climax and held there, teetering. He closed his eyes, muzzle ducking down, as he held himself back, muscles quivering as if he had hit several personal records in a single workout.

The bear snarled and pounded brutally as he roared over the edge, cock throbbing as it exploded into the wolf's rump, ropes of cum painting his passage and, finally, slickening his frantic, fervent thrusts. It was too little too late, however, as Si bet he would be sore for days – not that he cared. He melted into the bear's arms as he was used, scrabbling his claws over the wall to retain his balance the best he could, though his calves trembled with the effort of balancing on his toes.

As he pumped a hot, creamy load into his pup's tail hole, Mike nipped the wolf's shoulder– their little signal – and Si howled as he was permitted release. He jerked his head to the side and thrust wildly into the bear's paw as hot ecstasy burned up his body, hackles raising from the sheer forcing rocking him. He was no longer in control of his muscles and they twitched with a mind of their own, cock jerking and throbbing as it painted the back wall white with cum. A smaller load than the bear's, it was nevertheless impressive, and the wolf ground back to feel Mike's softening cock in his rump and his own swollen knot pushing insistently against his partner's paw. It was a sensation he craved for every night of the rest of his life. If he could be so lucky.

Maybe...there would be something more? Dragging in breath after much needed breath, Si looked back at Mike with a tired yet inherently satisfied grin.

"Hello?"

The cubicle door swung open and knocked into Mike's back, throwing him off balance and on top of the panting wolf. They crashed to the floor, Si tucking his head to the side at the last moment so as not to slam it into the wall, Mike's head whipping around in alarm. A startled red fox with black tips to his ears froze in the doorway, a bottle of shampoo clutched feebly in one paw. The paw on the towel around his waist tightened on the fabric as he took a step back, eyes fixed on the action before him. Mike's cock slipped in a splatter of cum from Si's tail hole, gaping slightly as if in lasting invitation.

The bear smirked cockily, quickly regaining his composure. As if sensing the adversary, a challenger that would decimate him in an instant, the fox swallowed hard and took a step back, ears flicking uncertainly. There was no right thing to do in the moment. Something nudged the back side of the towel – the side against the fox's fur – and Mike's leer grew, lips tugging up.

"Get out or join in," Mike growled, the invitational threat rumbling in the air between them.

Panting harshly, he parted his jaws in a grin that was more terrifying than encouraging, sharp teeth glinting with moisture.

"I warn you though. I don't raise *my* tail."

The New Guy

The after-five crowd was one of the most interesting groups of fitness furs to watch at the gym. Looking to get in a quick, solid workout after the conclusion of their working day, they took on workouts not for the faint of heart. There were the usual female furs on the cardio machines, hardly working with enough intensity to break a sweat in their sports bras; they were just there to say they'd gone or, sometimes, to get a break from their families too. And then there were the muscle-furs, locked in a world behind their headphones as they worked through the stresses of the day. Others chatted and otherwise lounged around the gym, scurrying into classes as and when their group was called. An outsider could not be sure what exactly went on in these classes, though they appeared to involve a lot of shouting and somewhat suppressed laughter from the instructor.

One had to have a wickeder side to work in such an environment, let alone as a class instructor.

A white rabbit with ears standing straight up from his head signed his name at reception and darted into the gym, whiskers quivering fervently. With red eyes, he was an unusual sight and his lean figure drew more than one eye, clad in the dark gym shorts and a loose T-shirt, modest enough for a workout. He stood in the doorway with his eyes near bulging out of their sockets until a bull coughed into his paw, standing behind and wanting to get by; there wasn't enough room to squeeze his hefty stomach past.

Leaping out of the way as if he had been stung, the rabbit anthro scampered to the treadmill, starting it up and setting the speed with some measure of confidence, though his whiskers twitched. He eased into a light run, relaxing at last, and kept his eyes fixed on the numbers before his muzzle, covering distance slowly and surely as the minutes passed.

Taking it easy at the tail end of his cardio, core and supplementary workout day – he didn't do anything by half – Malcolm watched the rabbit intently. With a jet-black coat, the stallion had a white triangle sliced over his shoulders, striking through a section of his mane, and a white stripe down the centre of his face. Malcolm's left leg was garbed in a white, equine sock, stretching above his fetlock, and he grunted as he worked through a set of Russian twists, sitting on his rump and twisting his torso from one side to the other, leaning back so that his weight was on his glutes.

The stallion's gaze went unnoticed as the rabbit bounced from hind paw to paw on the treadmill, his stride confident and lengthy. He covered an impressive distance without puffing for breath and Malcolm's ears twitched, swivelling to catch the thud, thud, thud of his paws slapping the running belt. There were those that said he was a little bit too curious around new members at the gym but, truly, he simply liked to lend a helping paw. Who didn't? And the rabbit, as cardio-fit as he was, was slim and lean when it came to any muscle development whatsoever.

And perhaps he was a little curious too...

Patiently, Malcolm waited out the rabbit for a solid half hour, running through an extended version of his routine with the familiarity of a well-versed lover. Crunches and sit ups came with ease while leg raises and oblique twists worked up a sheen on his darker coat, red shorts sticking to his legs. He went without a shirt at the gym during the summer months, finding the top floor establishment sweltering without adequate air conditioning. Such was the woe of a leisure centre gym that it bloomed with heat, wherever one found the centre in which to exercise. Malcolm could only be thankful that it had all the equipment he needed and not only that silly Smith machine and fixed weight barbells. This one was actually suitably designed with racks, his favourite piece of equipment.

Others, however, were not as keen to leap to the heavy weights when kinder, gentler machines beckoned sweetly, promising an easy fix to long-term effort. The rabbit slowed and hopped off the treadmill, sweeping his gaze from left to right as if the next phase of his routine would smack him upside the head, direction lost. Malcolm smiled and rose to his hooves as he replaced a nine-kilo medicine ball on its rack. Now was his time.

He clip-clopped up to the rabbit with a wink and flick of his tail that the rabbit eyed suspiciously, nose twitching as if he suspected some ulterior motive lay beneath the approach. Malcolm spread his paws wide in welcome, hoof-tipped fingers curled in slightly. What hidden motive could he ever have to introduce himself to a new gym-goer?

"Hey," Malcolm greeted the rabbit with a friendly smile. "Not seen you around before. Are you new here?"

The rabbit's back stiffened.

"Uh...yeah," he ducked his head, speaking only after a pause as if to collect his thoughts. "Yeah, I guess I am. New."

"That's cool. I'm Malcolm."

He offered his paw and the rabbit shook it with a weak grip, fluffy tail shuddering. It was often difficult for furs to hide emotion when their bodies were all so keen to naturally divulge in silent communication. It made it all the easier to read those who believed they were being discreet. And the bunny was far from discreet.

"I'm Tommy," the rabbit replied – there was not much harm in divulging a name. "Just signed up last week. Seems like a pretty nice place." He offered after a pause.

"What are you working on?"

Some of the tension left Tommy's shoulders and he rolled them backwards just the once, shrugging off the pressure of the meeting.

"Figured I'd come in to build some muscle, but not too much, you know. I like to run." He grimaced. "Ripped works for some, not me. I don't want to get big. And I don't do drugs."

Malcolm raised an eyebrow.

"Drugs?"

The rabbit's eyes went wide he took a step back, holding up his paws as if he was afraid Malcolm would advance on him for the mere suggestion that he was using frowned upon drug supplements.

"Not that I think you do drugs!" He added quickly, blushing beneath his fur, visible only for the presence of the lighter than light hairs. "Gosh, I didn't mean that at all, I swear!"

"Oh, relax," Malcolm laughed, drawing the eye of a lion with a full mane drinking from the water fountain. "There are some like that but...to each their own really. I stick to protein powder and creatine, maybe pre-workout if I'm going through a rough spot. I like to work to however I'm feeling and take it from there."

"Pre-workout?" Tommy wrinkled his nose. "Sounds...interesting."

Malcolm chuckled, raking his fingers through his mane.

"It's just to get some more energy into you before a workout, nothing sinister," the horse explained, tail swishing comfortably. "Could think of it like caffeine, just a bit different, careful not to have too much. But about that building muscle... You're gonna have to do a bit more than running on the hamster wheel to get that going for you."

The rabbit tilted his head, ears flopping to the side so that the very tips brushed his shoulder.

"I do? But I don't want big muscles. I mean, you look fricking *awesome* but I dunno if I have that kinda time to put into the gym."

Though he glowed from the compliment, Malcolm shook his head, endeavouring to point the rabbit in the right direction. There was never any point to be had in spinning one's wheels, believing a workout that was inherently wrong would have a specified result.

"It takes an hour a day, a few days per week," he said. "Not so bad, just about working smart."

The rabbit consider the notion for a moment; Malcolm could almost see the cogs whirring in his head, working overtime as he struggled to form words into a thought that was barely begun.

"Can you..."

The rabbit hesitated, back ramrod straight. Malcolm waited for the words that were music to his ears each and every time.

"Can you show me a few things? Just to get started? Please?" Tommy blurted, twisting his fingers together. "I really want to look good...get the ladies interested. I already got contacts sorted so I wouldn't have to wear glasses anymore, but nobody is interested when I look like a stick insect. They want someone...who looks like they are stronger."

He folded his arms firmly over his chest and looked away, ears drooping. The equine imagined him at home alone, sitting in front of the glare of a computer screen in the darkness, glasses perched upon his nose and a MMORPG open for the Wednesday night raid. Malcolm wouldn't have minded that himself, considering his raid ground had disbanded, but maybe something like that in the rabbit's life just wasn't suiting him quite right anymore. Fact was that the rabbit had decided to make a change yet was stuck as how to put an idea into action.

It won't be like that for much longer, little bunny. Not if I have anything to say about it.

"Sure, I will," he replied easily. "No worries at all."

"Really?" The rabbit perked up, bouncing on his toes. "You'd be willing to help me out?"

Malcolm nodded, cheered by the rabbit's reaction. It was nice to be appreciated. It was good to be able to help out as one stubborn tiger had once done for him. Payment for help received was still of the same currency, of course.

He still missed that tiger. And that back room at their gym where no one but them had dared venture.

Gesturing for the rabbit to follow, Malcolm led him into the weights room, planning on the fly to run him through a simple full body routine to begin, or at least cover a few of the required lifts. It was easiest to build strength from a base point, but the rabbit did not have any base to work from. He was a clean slate, a perfect candidate for beginners strength. Tommy beamed and bounced on the balls of his paws as they stood next to a half rack with an adjustable bench already set up beneath a racked bar from its previous user.

"Wow, even my friends wouldn't help me out like this, thank you! How can I ever repay you?"

The horse shook his head, mane falling to either side of his finely arched neck.

"Don't sweat it. Though they can't be very good friends if they won't lend a paw when you need it."

Malcolm adjusted the safety pins on the vertical beams of the rack down one notch – they would catch the bar if Tommy was tired enough to let it go in the middle of a lift – and the bar hooks one notch. The ring of metal on metal settled his soul and he nodded encouragingly to Tommy as he sat down on the bench, spreading his hooves comfortably. He laid back and demonstrated his first lift with just the Olympic bar, weighing in at a neat twenty kilos.

"This is a bench press. It's one of your staples for upper body," he imparted, experience strong in his tone. "Watch how I do it. Paws up to the bar."

Tommy nodded and observed carefully as Malcolm lifted the bar from the hooks as if it weighed nothing at all, bending his elbows to bring it down to his chest and up again, perfectly horizontal and grazing his chest as he dropped it. He repeated the motion to clearly demonstrate the lift to Tommy, explaining what the rabbit should be focusing on throughout the motion.

"Now, you try."

Cautiously, as if afraid the bench would nip his behind, Tommy laid himself down on the bench and raised his paws to the bar. As he lifted the bar, his arms quivered and it easily dropped to his chest, bumping into bone with undue force. Wincing, the rabbit struggled to raise it again and Malcolm stepped over him to help him push it back to the hooks, surprised by Tommy's initial weakness. He really was a blank slate when it came to fitness, or muscle building at least. Though it was unintentional, his stepping over the rabbit gave Tommy a clear view of his crotch and the bulge in the shorts as he leaned forward and took note of the rabbit's eyes on his maleness and not the bar he was supposed to be trying to lift.

Maybe there's more in this teaching thing than meets the eye... Excellent.

Malcolm swapped the twenty kilo Olympic bar for the ten-kilo training bar, assisting in the positioning of the clamps when weight plates were added. Tommy's ears drooped and he appeared so crestfallen at having to drop the weight that the horse stumbled over his words in his urgency to reassure his new friend.

"Hey now, come on – don't worry about it. Seriously," Malcolm implored, regaining Tommy's attention before he could descend into a full-on sulk. "It's just getting your body used to the motion. This bar will help with form, practice and warming up later, no matter what lift you're performing."

Tommy looked up hopefully, ears lifting just a little.

"Really?"

"Yes, really." Malcolm nodded encouragingly. "Now let's try that again."

They ran through the full scope of bench pressing and even added a scrap of weight when Malcolm was well and truly satisfied with the rabbit's form. Once that was complete, it was on to the other compound move for the upper body, overhead press, and the lower body squats that the rabbit found a little easier. His legs were stronger than his upper body, perhaps from running – though cardio burned more than it built – and he quickly had a basic squat form down pat, much to Malcolm's pleasure. It was a fine sight indeed to see a fur with their backside thrust back at him.

Deadlifts posed a greater challenge to the rabbit and Malcolm had him lift only forty kilos to give him a good base weight to work form and prevent him from tipping backwards accidentally from lack of weight. It was a strange lift requiring great concentration and secure form, lest one injure themselves, and it pleased him how studious Tommy was in learning the lift, even though sweat stained his T-shirt in a semi-circle beneath his arms. To tie off the first of his training sessions, Malcolm had him perform a simple barbell row, showing him how to keep his wrists from curling and work his back rather than any supporting muscles. It was tough going after the first lot of bench and overhead press and the rabbit was soon panting and sweating profusely.

"I reckon that's enough for today," Malcolm grinned. "You did good! You'll be able to start using these lifts yourself next time. Just don't be afraid to ask for help if you need it. Anyone's usually happy to lend a paw here."

The rabbit nodded, still working on catching his breath after concluding his final weighted set.

"Sure..." He took a breath. "Aren't you going to be around to help me anymore?"

"I can give advice, sure." Malcolm's ears pricked, only too happy to help out further. "I'm usually here from five to six, maybe six thirty on weekdays. When it comes to weekends, you can't tell with me. I'm a tad sporadic there."

He chuckled, amused by his own joke.

"Come on, let's head to the lockers and get changed. Done for the day and earned dinner good and proper, I reckon."

Tail flicking happily, Malcolm took the rabbit to the changing rooms, a small, enclosed space beyond the reception desk, which was currently unmanned. They ducked into the empty locker room and the rabbit hummed contentedly to himself, a theme tune that Malcolm would have bet his last workout on was from some video game or the other, something adventure roleplay-ish. But he hadn't found the time to get into the new ones; maybe that was something Tommy could recommend to him, later.

But there was no time to think about games and the implications of what a bunny was humming as he rummaged in his locker. The stallion licked his lips, nostrils flaring as he scented the air. It was time to put the next phase of his plan into action.

Snorting, Malcolm's eyes darkened and he tossed his head just a little, flipping his black and white mane to the other side of his neck to show off the fine arch and muscle beneath his thin coat.

"Hey."

"Hm?" Tommy turned his head and smiled, eyes warm and welcoming. "What's up?"

"Don't you think you owe me a little something for helping you out today?"

Scratching his cheek, the rabbit did not immediately understand and lifted a paw.

"I'm sorry, I didn't realise you charged," he attempted a joke. "What's the going rate for personal training these days? Or will you play ball with a mate's rate for little ol' me?"

The equine shook his large head slowly, tail flicking. Energy thrummed through him, though not from nerves, and his arousal swelled, pushing into the fabric of his shorts to tent it out in obvious testament to his virility. As if in slow-motion, the rabbit's eyes dropped to his crotch and Tommy's jaw dropped comically, gaping as if he was trying to catch flies with it. He held up his paws and backed into the lockers, pressing back as if he could disappear into them entirely if he only wished hard enough.

"Come on, bunny," Malcolm cajoled, tugging at the waistband of his shorts down to reveal the upper curve of his cock, bent down by its entrapment. "Don't think I haven't spotted you eyeing up my crotch through half this workout."

"I was watching your form!"

"Likely story," Malcolm retorted.

He advanced on the rabbit with a light smile on his lips. He only wanted some fun. The rabbit had nothing to worry about, nothing at all. And he had not yet run for the hills, so that had to say something. Placing his paws on either side of the rabbit's head, Malcolm held him to the lockers, penning him in with his muscled arms and chest with no chance of escape. Tommy shook his head desperately, eyes darting from side to side as his chest heaved.

"I want a girlfriend!"

Malcolm smirked, leaning in closer. The rabbit's pulse fluttered in his neck and he twisted his head to evade the equine's one looming in closer and closer.

"I'm sure of it. Doesn't mean you can't have a bit of fun on the side now though, does it?"

"Well...no." Tommy hesitated, meeting the equine's blue eyes with ones clouded with indecision and the faintest speculation of arousal. "It doesn't mean that, I guess."

Malcolm brushed his velvety equine lips over Tommy's neck, nipping an affectionate, sweet path up to the trembling line of his jaw.

"You straight, Tommy?" Malcolm asked him point blank: there was no point beating around the bush.

"Uh... Bi...maybe." Tommy shook his head, breath coming in shallow pants as the horse backed up against the lockers, equine bulge grinding into his less threatening one. "I dunno, I've never been with a guy before."

"Thought about it?"

Their lips were a hair's breadth apart, warm breath washing over the rabbit's muzzle. Tommy swallowed hard.

"*Yes.*"

Malcolm's lips crashed into the rabbit's and Tommy surrendered to his embrace, weak against the horse's chest. The rabbit's paws dropped and roamed Malcolm's bare chest, fingertips brushing over nipples that perked into hard peaks, arousal evident even there. The bulge in Malcolm's shorts grew and he tugged his shorts down enough to free his cock, letting the length spring free and slap against the rabbit's abdomen. As if following a choreographed routine, the rabbit wrapped his paw around the offered dick and, without any encouragement, stroked the full length gently, reverently. Malcolm groaned and rolled his head. It was almost too easy to persuade some.

"You're too obvious, Tommy," he told the rabbit, nipping his neck. "I saw you looking at me right from the time you entered the gym. You wanted me even then."

"I didn't..."

Tommy shook his head, denying it, for he had not even seen the horse until the hoofer had introduced himself. Yet it was easy to convince with the right words and tone of voice when so required.

There was no need for Malcolm to dig any deeper or plant further seeds, unless he considered a different kind of seed entirely. Placing a large paw gently on top of the rabbit's head, he guided him to his knees and drew him in close, shaft rubbing against Tommy's cheek as if in offering. Flushing crimson – the shade could be seen even through Tommy's fur, which was impressive in itself – the rabbit stuck his tongue out, closed his eyes and took the tiniest of licks. His tongue barely brushed the shaft before pulling back, but the first taste was all it took to bolster his confidence. One paw encircling the fat base of Malcolm's cock, behind the medial ring, Tommy parted his lips and suckled on the flat head, ears bolt upright from his skull.

Malcolm groaned and leaned heavily on one paw, palm flat against the locker above Tommy's head. Instinct told him to thrust but the more sensible part of his brain, often overruled, cautioned him against scaring off the rabbit too soon when he was such a keen, sweet soul. A muzzle could be trained and, if Malcolm had his way, he would be spending a lot more time with the rabbit, day after day and night after night. By the time he was finished with the bunny, Tommy would be a pro at lifting for health *and* at sucking cock.

Growing bolder, Tommy pushed his muzzle down the length of mottled horse cock, gulping rapidly as the head grazed the back of his throat. Pre-cum oozed from the tip and Tommy swallowed it down before it touched his tongue, eyes screwed up to peer down the length straining his lips wide. The corners of the rabbit's lips were struck through by a twinge from the unnatural stretch and he whimpered softly, bobbing his muzzle as he knew he enjoyed it himself. He had no other experience to go on but the gentle paw on his head was soothing and guided him through it, step by step.

"Easy now."

Malcolm stroked the rabbit's ears back down to his skull and scratched his cheek, soothing him from the sudden bout of nerves. Lapine muzzles, after all, were not suited to sucking horse cock. Though he had once met a female rabbit with such a penchant for sucking that she could have rewritten the book on fucking like bunnies. He smirked at the memory and rolled his hips, easing deeper into Tommy's muzzle as his throat worked overtime to swallow slick spurts of pre-cum. Malcolm was a particularly virile horse, but there was rarely a stallion that bucked that trend.

The rabbit pressed his cheek into the horse's paw as he sucked, staying still for Malcolm to thrust lightly between his lips. Down to the medial ring, the rabbit swallowed quickly and allowed his muzzle to be used as Malcolm wanted, letting the horse rock his hips, tail flicking, towards inevitable ecstasy. The equine huffed and stomped a hoof, release creeping up with an enticing smile and promise of greater pleasure, if only he would let himself go and *thrust*.

Malcolm, however, would not hurt his new friend and held back his natural urges, pleasure instead slowly building like water trickling into a jug until it had no choice but to overflow. He had no desire to suppress orgasm and the sweet, soft lips encasing his cock begged him to release, to fill the rabbit's slutty muzzle with a liberal dose of horse cum. Malcolm tossed his head and whinnied shrilly, nostrils flaring like those of a wild stallion.

The new guy was always the best.

He curled his fingers around the back of the rabbit's head and bucked, tail flagging high as the dam threatened to burst – and then did. Tommy closed his eyes as the equine's balls, forgotten in his delight of the thick shaft, near enough rumbled and sent cum throbbing down his length. The rabbit felt the rod of flesh between his lips quiver a second before the first rope of cum splattered into his mouth and throat and he convulsed, fighting the natural urge to cough as his gag reflex was hit. Somehow, he managed to keep himself under control and gulped down the horse's load quickly, throat working hard to keep up with the little jerks of Malcolm's hips and insistent, flared cock-head.

Grunting, Malcolm pressed his fingers into the rabbit's soft fur and snorted loudly as orgasm wracked his body, tail twitching as if in the height of summer when flies were a menace. With the slow build-up and lack of frenzied thrusting at the peak, climax squeezed every drop from him and he rocked forward, imagining driving into the rabbit's tight – of course, it would be tight – tail hole as the bunny cried out his name into the pillows. The horse groaned and came down from his high, looking down at Tommy with lust and speculation shining in his eyes. How would the rabbit feel to take? That sweet delight would come another time.

He withdrew his softening cock from Tommy's lips before his jaw became too strained and the rabbit moaned, the damp spot and bulge in his gym shorts showing that Malcolm had not been the only one to enjoy their locker room dalliance. Cum dribbled from the corner of Tommy's lips and the rabbit quickly licked it up, glancing shyly up at the horse that he had just become so intimately acquainted with, one paw lightly stroking his dropped, still eager member.

Looking down at the bunny licking horse cum off his muzzle, Malcolm grinned and tossed him his very own red towel. Perhaps with cum marking it irrevocably, the horse would remember to do some laundry later on that night. He smiled. It was still unlikely, though it would remind him of the fun had when he dragged it out of his bag, smelling of equine maleness the next day. That was what every horse's gym bag smelled like, right?

The door to the changing room opened and Malcolm swiftly tugged his shorts up, hiding his half-hard shaft from immediate sight as Tommy, as clean as he could be after a quick wipe of his muzzle, screwed the towel into a ball. Cheeks heated, he passed it sheepishly back to the equine and looked away, suddenly intrigued by the contents of the locker he had forgotten about.

Leaning in close, Malcolm pressed his chest to the rabbit's back and lipped one of his long ears softly, making him shiver. Tommy shyly peered back over his shoulder, muzzle brightened by a smile only the horse could see.

"I think we have a beautiful agreement going here," Malcolm whispered into Tommy's ear, so low that no one else could hear.

The rabbit's whiskers trembled and Malcolm stood upright, discreetly adjusting his shorts so they sat more comfortably. Winking, he blew the rabbit a cheeky kiss and turned away, tail flagging proudly over his muscled rump. He knew Tommy's eyes were on his ass – there was no way the rabbit was completely straight after this experience – and glowed from the silent praise. He should be wanted. He looked fucking *awesome*. Tommy had said so. And who was the horse to claim otherwise?

Gulping, Tommy raised his paw in shy farewell and conclusion to their little liaison, at least for the present day.

"Same time tomorrow?"

Stripes & Sweat

It was easy for Zane to lose himself when he was on the treadmill. Running did not come particularly naturally to him, being a tiger who was built more for short bursts of explosive speed rather than long-time running and marathon distances, but he knew it was good for him. That was where a lot of furry fitness in the gym came to, as so many different animals were built for different things – things that did not always match up as well as they might have liked with the lifestyle they had.

Desk jobs and factory work, even work that sent furs out into the forests and mountains beyond the cities… Everything came with different challenges and forced an anthro to adapt in a way beyond what their species may have naturally been capable of. But that was exactly why anthros like Zane were anthros and not like their feral, wild ancestors – the very ancestors that still roamed free, in most cases, even if their cognitive ability and their evolved bodies were very different.

Which was one way too in which Zane was different from the wild tigers he had needed to study, for his species-specific homework, way back when he'd been in school. He might have felt hot and cloying in the gym, as if his body was prickling all over with built-up heat, though tigers naturally chose to submerge themselves in water or be more active at night to avoid heating up too much.

When he had to look after his cardiovascular health, however, by running on the blasted treadmill, Zane was left with fewer options. He preferred weightlifting, with slow, controlled movements, challenging his body and training his mind as he focused. And that was really all there was to it. When he could take a break between sets, resting and thinking about how the motion, how the lift itself, had felt, everything felt peaceful, as if he was allowing his body to accept the stress on it, how the strain had broken muscle fibres and challenged them. He had not gone too much into the focus of weightlifting, in all honesty, for some did indeed treat it like a religion – and he respected that too. That was different, for him, even if he did like to let it all soak in.

Maybe it was a tiger thing.

What Zane did know, however, was that it all felt different on the treadmill. It was tedious and mind-numbing, no matter how many podcasts he listened to, working on his stride, step after step. It should have been rhythmic and soothing but, really, it was anything but that to him. All he was thinking about, as his trainer-clad feet slapped the moving surface, was getting off.

Or getting off in a different way. With his headphones hooked into his ears, orange-striped fur bright in the moderate lighting of the plain, bare-bones gym, the tiger could, at the very least, take in the eye candy. His tail, with a solid, dark tip, flicked back and forth as he ran, though Zane was sure it would not be all that obvious he was staring, trying to put on more of a blank-faced expression, as if he was zoning out and just staring off into the distance like so many others that headed onto the cardio equipment to get what they needed done.

There were plenty there in the gym that day, the cardio machines facing out on the space near the reception so he could see who was coming and going. There were the usual crowd there, for after work in the evening, but more were leaving than they were coming. Short and sweet gym workouts were in vogue, apparently, but Zane still liked to make the most of his time, especially considering he had to drive to the gym. Making the most of every second was important to him. Even if he would make the most of his time at home too by sprawling out on the sofa and flicking through his favourite YooToob channels.

Hey, a tiger didn't always have to change their stripes...

A meerkat sprang by, light on his feet even as he slung his gym bag over his shoulder. Zane didn't pay the ladies all that much mind, having always been with guys. He didn't think he'd ever like anyone else, though there had been a couple of non-binary anthros that had caught his attention too and thickened the bulge in his pants. He was open to trying, as long as he was attracted to the fur.

Big, muscular guys, however... Ah, that would always be the tiger's first choice of eye candy. He had to focus on his step on the treadmill just a little bit more, belatedly lamenting that he hadn't gone for the elliptical instead, for at least he had the handles to hold onto there, which steadied him. He'd slipped on the treadmill, embarrassingly, more than once before, because he hadn't been concentrating on his own workout. That didn't stop the feline from enjoying the view, however, for it was one of the only things that kept him on the treadmill.

A bear rubbed a towel over his paws, soaking up the sweat that had emerged from the glands. He was quick to leave, however, replaced by a stoat entering with a long-legged gait and a canny look in his eye that suggested that he was there to get in and get out, though he was a little on the slim side for Zane's tastes. The tiger nodded at the rhino who ducked in, heading to the dumbbell racks, recognising Stan, though they didn't have time for a chat that day. He appreciated the rhino's cannonball shoulders, however, shirtless as usual, and his slight muscle gut. There were many different body types, after all, that deserved the best kind of attention and Zane was not only interested in admiring those with leaner, high muscle body types. Heavy lifters often didn't look as lean as bodybuilders, but it depended on their species too.

Yet his attention landed on a big, black bull with a ropey, swinging tail, who was doing push-ups on the opposite side of the room, in an open mat area. He had been there for some time already, lifting in the rack room with barbells, though Zane had not been paying close enough attention to know what he was working on that day. If he was doing push-ups, perhaps he was doing chest and back?

What Zane could see was that he was sleek and shiny with sweat, his shirt off and his long, loose shorts still managing to show off his ass as he did push-up after push-up. His shoulders and biceps flexed to balance his weight, pressed up nicely onto his cloven hooves, though he didn't seem to be struggling at all. Or perhaps that was just Zane's perception of him, admiring the sweat glistening on the back of his neck, how his light grey horns complemented the shape of him with the matte appearance of them.

Bulls could sweat better than a tiger but not as efficiently as other creatures. It was enough, however, that the tiger's nose twitched, taking in that richer, muskier aroma of sweat where it rose from the skin, over most of the bull's body. Between his thighs and under his arms, as was the case often with their evolved species, had to be the most fragrant, and Zane was not ashamed in the slightest of taking a deep, appreciative breath. There was a lot of information to be contained in sweat and, more widely, general scents of the body too, though he wasn't thinking about that. He wasn't thinking of how the bull was, technically, a prey animal and how he was technically a predator.

All he could think about was how he wanted that stacked, muscular body on top of him, pinning him to the wall, fucking him right up under his tail.

Zane swallowed a growl, feeling his cock press out teasingly from his sheath, filling it out, even though he tried to shake off his arousal, to ignore it for the time being. Sure, yes, he could enjoy what he was looking at, though he could not just walk around the gym like a young thing with a stiffie. He hadn't even done that in his younger days, having a bit more class than that. Frankly, that was the sort of thing that he would only have thought of doing in his dreams and fantasies – and Zane knew exactly where those were supposed to reside.

"Mmph…"

The tiger grunted softly. His tail lightly hung, focusing on easing the tension in his body. His shaft slipped back down a little more but he didn't have to concern himself with that, as long as it was not obviously tenting out the front of his loose jogging bottoms. They were what he usually wore when heading to the gym, even if he had a T-shirt on that day too that was a little too tight across his chest, showing off the muscle definition there. When it got warmer still, he'd go down to shorts, just like the bull and others.

Still, he couldn't stop his eyes from going back to the bull, again and again, even grazing the bovine's gaze. There was just something about that casual ease of how he completed push-up after push-up, pressing through the motion and taking a break from time to time, swapping to pull-ups that practically put his natural bulge on full view to Zane.

"Ah, fuck…"

Zane chuffed a low laugh under his breath, his tail swinging back and forth. The pull-up bars faced the treadmills directly, yet the tiger swore that he caught something of a smile tugging at the bull's lips. Was he *teasing* him? Oh, he might well have been doing so, though the tiger wasn't all that sure what he was to do with that information. Sure, he'd been staring at the bull, wondering if he was going to feature in his fantasies later that night, but maybe, just maybe, it was possible some fun might be in hand before even then.

Well, a tiger could dream.

Sometimes, however, dreams came true. Raunchy, lustful, kinky dreams. For the bull smirked openly as he dropped down to the ground once more, landing heavily on his hooves with a decidedly larger bulge at his crotch than had been there when he'd first started doing pull-ups. Even though Zane knew that it was a cocky move, he hadn't seen the bull there before and threw caution to the wind, slowing down and hopping off the treadmill as the black bull approached.

He made a moment of it, grabbing his water bottle and rubbing his sweaty paws off with his towel, even if his eyes were on the bull. Every nerve ending in his body sang with heat but he didn't want to consider cooling off anymore, more interested in warming up, seeing if something could be kindled between him and a certain bull.

Luckily for him, the bull came straight up to him, his ears twitching, though he supposed that bovines could not prick their ears like canines. Communication through body language tended to be quite subtle between different species, even though Zane was interested in just how the bull was going to communicate with him, even if the gleam in his eye was tempting the tiger to consider just how much the bull was promising him.

Hey, he could have his hopes…

Zane smiled as pleasantly as he could with his heart pounding, sure that the bull could hear it too.

They were sensitive like that, though the bull's eyes dropped subtly, just once, before flicking back up to his face.

"Hey," the bull said. "I'm Russell, or Russ, either works. Seems this is a pretty nice gym, I just joined."

Oh, small talk?

That much he could work with!

"It is," Zane said, his tail swishing with just a little bit too much enthusiasm. "Name's Zane, been coming here a while. How are you finding everything here?"

Their conversation was normal, flicking back and forth naturally between them, flowing more easily and naturally than he could have imagined things going with anyone Zane was meeting for the first time. But it was not normal to have his skin prickling like that, wanting to put his back up by raising his shoulders, his tail curling and twisting back and forth. It was not normal, though very much desired, to have so much tension crackling openly in the air between them, so much so that another friend of Zane's from the gym, a snow leopard, threw him a questioning look. A thumbs-up from the leopard, however, told the tiger all that he needed to know about what others saw there.

Well, it wouldn't be the first time two guys had gotten a little freaky in the showers or the changing rooms… Or even around the back of the gym…

"Are you going to come back here again soon then?" Zane asked, picking up on a thread of conversation that, for a moment, had dropped between them. "You know, if you're away with work and stuff."

The tiger wasn't sure just how much of the conversation he had been focusing on, not as his eyes had drifted, roaming curiously all over the bull, wondering just what that body would feel pressed against his. His tail lashed and lashed, simply unable to keep it still, and Russell noticed that too, coming in a little closer, the bulk of his body blocking the tiger from the rest of the gym. And any escape too… Though that was a good thing, for him, making the ropes and twists in his stomach squirm into overdrive, a flicker of something that Zane had not felt in a long time rising within him.

Oh, fuck, yes…

He could take what he wanted – especially if it was under his tail. Russ pressed in briefly, just enough to trail the back of his paw over Zane's rising hard-on. When the tiger did not flinch away but gave another throaty chuff, rolling his hips, they both knew just where the unspoken understanding lay between them, as clear as day.

And that was just how they ended up fumbling their way down to the back of the gym and into the staff-only area. It was only a short hallway with some doors leading off from it, storage closets with cleaning equipment and some stuff from the gym that was not currently in use, but it was enough for them. Enough for them to stumble against one another as soon as they were out of the public line of sight, grunting softly, licking their lips, though the deep, guttural tones emitted between them only rose once they were sure that they wouldn't be seen back there.

"Unff… Fuck, I didn't think getting to a new gym would start this well," Russ groaned as the tiger leaned him back against the wall, his tongue brushing crudely up against his bare throat. "Ah… Does this always happen at this gym?"

Zane chuffed a laugh, grinning, eyes creasing slightly at the corners with his horny amusement.

"More often than you'd think, but it's been a while for me…"

"Oh?"

Russ grinned, palming the front of the tiger's jogging bottoms, the soft, flowing fabric not leaving anything to the imagination as the rise of his cock swelled eagerly into the bull's touch. It knew where it was needed, very much so, and the bull groaned as his palm was filled with throbbing flesh, even if the tiger had soft barbs on his cock too. They were softer and more pliable, thicker and fleshier too, than those of his wild ancestors, but they were not going to be going into the bull's tail hole that day, no. Not when the tiger melted against him, running his paws over Russ' chest, feeling the shape of his pecs, how deliciously brawny he was.

"Mmmph… Yeah," Zane said, the words coming thickly from the back of his throat, as if he was having to push them from his lips with his tongue, each and every time. "Just didn't find a guy to hang with, didn't have the time…"

Russell grinned.

"Well, you have the time now. But I didn't expect you to purr quite this sweetly for me…"

Zane allowed himself to be roughly handled, leaning into the attention even as he tried to be as outwardly compliant as possible. He just wanted to show him he was into everything, even if he was chuffing lowly and grunting, words lingering on his lips that were spent in moans.

"Mmmph… Yes…"

He turned to face the wall and Russ dragged his shirt over his head, relieving him of the tight fabric, for which he was more than grateful. His jogging bottoms went next as Zane braced on the wall, though the bull was already pulling down his own shorts, exposing his erection. His hard-on sprang up into a needy touch, and he panted heavily through his nostrils, snorting and blowing out hard.

His shaft, however, was not like the tiger's. It was bigger, longer by about an inch – though it was not as if anyone was going to measure it at such a time. That moment was only about pleasure and nothing more than that, two guys taking what they so very crudely needed from one another in the back of the gym. Maybe they'd get caught or maybe they wouldn't, but he was sure that they would get away from it. Zane, after all, had gotten a blowjob a couple of months back in the gym showers and the staff were well-used to turning a blind eye to the antics of those that liked to really wind down after their workouts.

So, it was okay for him to roll his hips back and take the hot slide of that cock up against his backside, even though his glutes were hard after a leg workout the day before, still pumped up. Damn, how he loved the pump. He flicked his tail up, the heat of a blush tickling across the fur of his cheeks and neck, even if it could not be seen through his fur. Maybe if someone was stroking his face, sure, but the bull was busy running his paws, with the chunky, hoof-like fingertips and thick, blocky nails, down the tiger's sides to his hips, groping and squeezing, teasing him with all that he could get from his body.

"Mmmph…"

"Easy there, tiger," Russ chuckled throatily, sliding down behind him. "Ever had a tongue up there before? Let me get you ready. You okay with that?"

"Ah, fuck, yes…"

It had been a while indeed since he had been rimmed and he didn't need to be prepared, though he appreciated the bull's care too in attending to him. It could have been nothing more than a quick and raunchy fuck that left him wobbly-legged and drained of his cum but Russ seemed keen to make it even more than that. For lust could be played out in the most tantalising, intoxicating of ways as he humped and ground his hips back, panting lightly, the bull's thick, fleshy tongue tracing over his ass.

"Ah... Yes..."

"Mmm..."

The bull leaned in closer, taking his time, as if they weren't only fucking in the back of the gym, storage racks around them, using the bare bit of wall in the storage room to lean against. That was helpful, at least to them, and the light buzzed and flickered dimly above, as if it was about to go out. The half-light made everything seem a little dirtier and seedier than before, yet it was a clawing, driving edge he rather liked, pressing his forehead into the cool of the wall.

Russell was soft with him, however, despite his bulk, despite his muscle. Standing, the bull would have been taller than him, a little more so with the horns too, but he could be just as powerful and dominating down on his knees with his tongue slurping over Zane's backside. His tongue skilfully wriggled up against the tiger's sensitive pucker, lapping over in long, teasing strokes. Zane's toes curled, claws coming out as he kicked his trainers off, his joggers stuck on one ankle.

"Ah... Ohhh..."

Russell groaned into his backside, though there was only so much he could do in terms of speaking. His muzzle was rather otherwise occupied.

He grunted against Zane and the tiger quivered, letting every moment wash over and through him, the wet tickle of that tongue flicking over his tail hole delicious. It made him quiver, his legs apart and bracing, the textured edges of his hole twitching and pulling as he clenched down. Though he didn't want to clench too hard and stop the bull from penetrating him with the wet slurp of his tongue, letting Russ inside as he pressed deep with a single, devious lap. He moaned, trying to muffle his cries and to be as quiet as possible, though if they were going to get caught then they were going to get caught. It didn't matter just how loud or how quiet they were, in the end, because they could enjoy each other there, exactly the way they were.

"Unff..."

It was so good and so deep... A tongue curling up inside him, lapping as if it was seeking out his prostate. That would take, in his case, a couple of digits pushed up inside him to find the right spot. But he still very much appreciated the lap and the slide of a skilled tongue like that, how it pulled over his ring, dragging and sliding. It wasn't like any other tongue that he'd enjoyed in his tail hole before, sweeping around his anal ring as it pulled out and then drove back in, slickening him up nicely.

It was all that he needed, panting heavily, his tail flicking back and forth, hiked high so that his need was apparent. His cock was out, but, for the moment, it was not the main event as he grunted, licking his lips. It may have throbbed and pulsed deliciously, though he needed it more, grinding back ardently onto that tongue, the bull's soft muzzle shoved between his rear cheeks.

The bull groaned deeply against him and Zane shuddered, enjoying even that soft reverberation flowing through him, how it made his backside ache a little more for the main event. He wanted it – and somehow the bull knew that too. Even without words.

He felt the bull stand behind him, almost lamenting the loss of his tongue. But he ached for more, the bull grinding up against him, sliding his smooth, thick length between the tiger's glutes.

"Mmm, you taste so fucking good," he hissed, pushing his muzzle over Zane's shoulder as the tiger leaned into him, braced on the wall with his hips thrust back as much as he was able. "You ready for this? Not got any real lube or anything…"

"Nah, it's all good," Zane grunted, trying to stay still, even as his body wanted desperately to hump and thrust, need coursing through him with every beat of his heart. "Fuck me… I'll tell you if it's too much."

Yet that was enough. That was enough, all in a good way, the best of ways, the rounded, slightly tapered, head of Russ' cock grinding up under his tail. He kept his tail up as high as he could for him so that Russell could grip it and present it in just the right spot, then and only then rolling his hips to slowly but surely spread the tiger's ass open.

Zane howled. He couldn't help himself and there was nothing at all there he wanted to hold back, trying to hump and grind, though he was forced to stay there, to brace. If he didn't, he wasn't going to get every inch of cock rammed up inside him that he wanted – and he wanted every fucking inch that the bull had on him. He needed it all, stretching him out patiently, deliciously. And he felt it too, the bull caring for him with the long, languid thrust of his hips, penetrating him deeply, stretching him out, giving him the time for his tail hole to accept that hot length, two bodies coming together as one.

And no more words were needed. Not in that moment, not when they were more than accepting of each other's actions, panting and heaving, sweat and musk painting the air. Without their clothes, they were just as they were, with nothing to differentiate them, truly, from any other bull or tiger. Why, they could even have been anonymous, though it would turn out, in the end, they would stay in touch later, something building between them that went beyond their lust for the gym.

And that was okay, exactly the way that it was, panting, heaving, their bodies rolling lustfully together, somewhat in time. The bull took control, dominating him easily, thrusting and grinding, drawing back only a few inches so that he could have the delight of penetrating the tiger's backside all over again. He huffed hotly, nostrils fluttering, but the carnal nature of their bodies coming together was all that was needed right then and there, sweat glistening on his hide, despite the warmth brimming over inside him.

Zane's paws braced on the wall, sweaty and slick. His musk rose but it was the grasp of the bull's paw around his cock that him mewling and yowling, torn between being higher-pitched and deeper, rougher, coassr, as he was more often. If he was not dominating right then, then maybe there was something for him there, something that he could lust for. There was passion there, a sense of giving up a part of himself to the bull, his tail curling and twisting back against the bull's stomach.

"Unff... Russ..."

He wasn't usually one to cry out a partner's name while having sex, though it felt right. It felt like it was meant to be, his glutes tense, squeezing around the cock in his ass to the best of his ability. Russell grunted and thrust a little harder, his hips slapping Zane's backside with every thrust.

Mmmm...

He'd gotten every inch of his dick into Zane's backside. Now, that was something to be proud of, for it was not as if he had planned for their fun to happen, better able to relish in the moment. He didn't want to miss a thing as the bull's thrusts grew increasingly savage, as if he was submitting to his pleasure too, even if he was in a position of control.

And that was okay too, as long as he was taking care of the bottom of the situation too, Zane. He panted heavily, hot breath washing over the tiger's shoulder as his head thrust over, a tongue lashing out teasingly against Zane's cheek. Zane groaned, yet that paw worked over and over his cock, pumping up and down, and there was only so much he could do as tension built in his loins, hotter and harder than ever before.

Of course, that had to be an exaggeration. And he should have thought just a little bit more about where he was cumming as the bull forced him closer and closer, that heat rising, thick and fast. It was coming whether he was ready for it or not and it was not even for Zane to contain it in the moment, but…well…neither of them. They just had to let it fly, the bull's fingers folding over the barbs, pulling and tugging, though the barbs were still soft enough on his cock that they did not catch uncomfortably on the bull's paw.

Yet he lost himself there, thrusting, humping, torn between grinding back onto Russ' cock and thrusting forward into the hold of his paw. His cock erupted, sending long, thick spurts of cum out to paint the wall. The tiger did not even look down, too caught up in the rolling throbs of ecstasy powering through him, giving himself up to the wild beast of climax. There was nothing there in which he had to hold back, heaving and panting, the bull thrusting harder, the slap of his hips bouncing off the tiger's ass faster and more urgent than before.

And yet the bellow of the bull creaming inside him was more delicious than even his own orgasm, Russell leaning over him heaving, trusting Zane to take the weight of his body. Zane heaved and panted, letting the bull's cream fill him up, though some still drooled and slopped out around the length of his cock, where the join of their bodies tightened. He clenched around him, squeezing deviously, though he didn't want to do more, to hinder the moment.

It was all about enjoying the moment, exactly as it was, even if neither the bull nor the tiger yet knew what was to come of it, whether they were going to get something even more passionate than what they had experienced there. Muscles bulged and the scent of sweat and musk and sex tangled together in the air: a delicious cocktail for Zane's senses. Still, physical strength could be subdued and cared for too, which was just where the domination and submission of a moment exactly like that came into play. At least, for Zane.

"Mmm…"

He purred throatily, letting his head hang as the bull grunted, remaining deep inside him while he spent every last drop of his seed. Those balls finally trembled up against his backside as Russ pressed in, though he hoped to feel even more of them, in the days and weeks to come.

Lust, after all, could turn into something else. From fuck buddies to lifting buddies to just buddies…and then something more again.

With sweat and stripes, passion taking them in hand, Zane and Russell had a world of possibilities before them.

Lean Legs

Ari huffed, the hare relaxing into his stride, focusing only on the slap of his large hind paws on the treadmill with every stride. It was easy for him, though he did not have long-distance endurance: that was something Ari was building up to. His brown-grey fur darkened in patches, under his arms and, under his shorts, around his crotch between his legs too, with sweat, though the hare was just hitting his stride. Sweating was a part of going to the gym, Ari knew. Even though he would not have honestly been going if not for the little belly pooch that had grown as he moved into his thirties.

Damn… The hare really wished he could still eat like he was in his thirties. But, as he leaned into his stride on the treadmill, his long shorts brushing against his legs, coming down to the narrowest point of his quadriceps, Ari knew it was alright. He could keep going and he could relax into everything, moment by moment, simply letting the rhythm of his own paws carry him onward.

However, he saw he'd caught someone's eye. It was not unexpected, as there were rather a lot of sidelong looks in the gym, though most kept themselves to themselves. A hare, on the other paw, would always notice the intense, brooding stare of a wolf, boring into him, as if he was prey.

Of course, predator and prey relations were no longer issues: thankfully, that was something that had been sorted out more or less globally five or six centuries ago, for which herbivores were exceedingly grateful. His tail twitched, fed through the hole in the back of his shorts, though Ari studiously kept it moderately placed, not wanting to flip it up and show a white flash of warning. It was an old instinct that didn't really have any place in his life anymore, but hares and rabbits were particularly likely to fall prey to it. It could also be used as a threat, flipping the tail up.

Wolves didn't see it like that though and, as he ran, slowing his pace a little towards the end of his cardio session, Ari met the wolf's eyes. Tall and grey, he was a few inches, perhaps three, taller than the hare, his vest-top leaving little to the imagination when it came to his muscular chest and broad pectoral muscles. A slash of white fur dove into the neckline of his vest, though it was clear he was only wearing it for comfort. It was an interesting contrast to Ari, who had gone bare-chested that day. In a gym like that, it was pretty much accepted for guys and non-binary folk to go without anything on their upper bodies, as many of the lady furs were in sports bras anyway.

It was better to be comfortable. And yet Ari was far from comfortable as he ran, heat pooling deliciously in his stomach. He licked his lips, cocking his head lightly, though the tilt of his ears made it look like he was tipping his head more than he actually was.

The wolf grinned, a shine of light entering his amber gaze, which had not been there before. Ari's heart surged, lifting, and the hare shared his smile.

It was funny how a note of attraction could be shared like that, without any words being exchanged. Of course, it was entirely up to Ari to get off the treadmill and stretch in front of the wolf in the open section of the gym, making sure he got to see every flexed muscle and the flat tone of his stomach, which had, at least, melted away under his cardio regime. The wolf, on the other paw, was all brawn and bulk, though the wag to his tail was particularly enticing, suggesting a softer side that the hare ached to sink into.

"Are you going to follow me out to my car without even giving me a name then?" Ari murmured, pointing his ear in the wolf's direction with the tiniest flicker of a smile on his lips, seductively discreet. "That would be rather rude, don't you think?"

The wolf smirked, raising an eyebrow as he leaned back against the wall.

"Well, it would have been ruder to follow you out without checking you were interested first," the wolf said, running his tongue along the side of his muzzle. "Name's Neil... And, yeah, I'm game, cutie."

It was rare for a first meeting to go that well, although, well...hm... It was not as if Ari was unused to meeting guys quite like that. Always with a condom though, of course, just to make sure he was okay. And he'd rather run the risk of getting caught than head into a location that was too secluded, putting himself at risk of harm.

There were many fun things to be undertaken, with others, as long as an individual was sensible about it... And the hare always had friends who knew where he was and a roommate amenable to a quick text to know when to expect him back.

That was just how Ari ended up with his paw shoved down the wolf's shorts, grasping his swelling hard-on, around the back of the gym, behind Ari's car. He didn't know where Neil's ride was, but it didn't matter, not as the bigger male grunted and thrust into his paw, leaking pre-cum all over. It was the hare, however, who was in control and the wolf didn't need to be dominant under those circumstances, not as Ari grinned widely and folded his ears smoothly back.

"Mmm... Oh, I do like those whines you make. Do you have any more for me?"

Neil grunted, trying to swallow a moan, but there was still a laugh on the wolf's lips as he thrust divinely into the hare's paw. He was nice and thick too, in a way that Ari would not have minded having stretching out his tail hole, but a bit of preparation before taking a cock like that most likely would not go amiss.

He wondered if the wolf would switch with him too, enjoying the pleasure of both sides, flipping back and forth. Leaning over him as he gently powered into the muscled stud's backside would not go amiss. That was, if they wanted to meet up again after that saucy first time…

The future did not matter, however, only that they were there taking pleasure from one another, Ari trembling as Neil swallowed a grunted curse. The wolf's cock was so intoxicating, the sort of dick he wanted to work his paw up and down slowly, teasing and edging him, drawing out the pleasure for as long as possible.

They didn't have that time, unfortunately, behind the gym. They did have a moment, however, and maybe that moment in itself was more than enough for them to get to know one another.

Neil groaned, licking his lips, trying not to make too much noise. Not because the wolf didn't want to, of course, but as he didn't want to draw any unwanted attention to himself. He wouldn't have wanted, after all, them to be interrupted in the middle of everything, his pink tongue lolling out over his soft, grey lips.

It was good to be given attention like that. No one else had caught his eye recently and, truth be told, Neil was going through something of a dry spell. That was okay though, for it was not as if everyone was out there having sex all the time, despite how some made it out to be. He leaned back against the car that he didn't own, relishing in sensation, the crisp night air brushing his coat, though a streetlight cast a pool of artificial light near them, the spill of it not touching them.

So, they could remain tucked away in their darkness, hidden in lust, need rising, flowing smoothly through them with every beat of their hearts. Ari murmured something to him, licking his lips, though Neil didn't quite catch what he said, even if it did not matter.

"Easy now… You're going to blow so quickly, aren't you?"

Ari would not even need to get down on his knees to suck off the wolf, the hare thought with a smirk, though he'd been angling for that anyway. Neil's tail swung back and forth lightly, not quite wagging, as he nipped at his lip, trying to bear through the pleasure so that he did not cum quite so quickly.

Yet the issue there was that they had to be swift too, the notion that someone could come upon them with their groans mingling more enticing than it had any right to be. Ari had challenged that, time after time again, though he had never got caught. He wasn't sure still whether he wanted to be caught in the act or not. Maybe the idea was hotter than the reality.

He squeezed the wolf's dick, another dribble of pre-cum sliding slickly down his cock, marking his paw. The wolf whined, eyes wide, plaintive, though he made no move at all to take his pleasure into his own paws. Ari liked that. He liked that rather a lot, in fact, playing the balance of power into his favour, willingly and seductively.

Neil definitely deserved a reward for that.

"Cum for me then," Ari hissed. "You don't want anyone to see us out here with my paw down your pants, do you? Hm? Or maybe you'd like that…"

The wolf grunted and twisted, though he only thrust more urgently into the hare's paw, Ari's fingers curled around him, brushing the rise of his rapidly swelling knot. He would not take long at all, but that was just how the hare liked it, letting those panting moans rise and rise, filling the air, a swell of passion in how hard his cock throbbed against him.

"Mmm, come on then… Don't have much time…"

Neil grunted, his tail lifting, as if he was flagging it like a horse. But it was merely stiffening at that raunchy point of climax, when he thrust and spilt his seed. His cock may have still been mostly pinned back within his shorts still, the head poking out, but he should really have been more careful about where he was spending his seed. Ropes of thick, rich cum splattered the front of his shorts, an errant spurt marking Ari's car, though neither of them cared about that. At least Neil could dart back to his own car quickly enough, not having to walk about with obvious cum streaking his clothes.

"Unff… Ah… Wow…"

The wolf's tail softened a little, wagging, but the orgasm was not the main event there, oh no. It was the risk, the lure of something new, the chance that there could be a little more between them. He grunted and shook his head, though Ari softly took his weight against him, letting the wolf lean into him. Even though Neil was taller than him, he had him steadied and could support him, even if Neil put his full weight on him.

It was a moment… and yet a moment, even with the high of orgasm, could be so much more too.

"If you think you're bold enough to repay the favour," Ari said, tucking a card with his name and number on it into the wolf's pocket, "my number's on there. Give me a ring. Or not. But then we'll know just who has the upper paw here…"

Neil groaned, still engaged with tucking his softening shaft back into his shorts, though it would take a while yet for his knot to fully deflate. That was just something the wolf was going to have to live with on the drive home.

"Oh, you can bet I never go without reciprocating."

The hare's lean legs, after all, had already drawn Neil in, and the wolf would soon find himself down on his knees, worshipping Ari's cock, while need swelled between them.

A quickie outside the gym, in the end, could turn out to have a beautiful end indeed…

A Swimmer's Body

Kody exhaled sharply, breaking from the surface of the Olympic swimming pool in a spray of water and air, tiny droplets flying from his lips and fur. The red fox shook his head, bobbing in the water, his chest heaving faintly from the level of exertion he had put his body through. Swimming was much better exercise for him rather than the weightlifting that he only did one day a week, preferring the long, lean laps, the cardio that made him feel as if he was slipping away into another world every time he eased into the water.

When the fox was underwater, his fur floating and streaming around his body as if it was no longer weighed down by the bounds of gravity or even the natural oils in his fur, he was free. Kody often headed down to the ocean, and out to lakes also, to dip into free swimming – wild swimming, some called it. It was a dangerous hobby, considering that a pool was an enclosed, safe environment when one could never otherwise be quite sure what lay under the surface elsewhere, yet it had hooked him from his teens. And when Kody sank his teeth, metaphorically, into something, there was little that could get the vulpine to let go.

Like the coyote he had taken to hanging out with, flirting, fucking – the usual for their kind. Not their species, of course, but just their type of guy. They enjoyed the pool and built smooth, lean muscle down the lines of their bodies, but they would never do it competitively or for anything other than the pure enjoyment of it. Why, even the aspect of physical fitness it helped with was a side thing to just liking to be in the water.

Kody, however, enjoyed pinning Shane up against the lockers even more, growling and nipping sharply at the coyote's neck while the slutty little thing ground back against him. He was such a tease... And that had been the way the first time they had hooked up too, the coyote bent over into the back of Kody's car while the fox railed him, leaving him good and sore under his tail. Really, even for a quickie, there were few better ways to get fucked.

The fox licked his lips, the faint taste of chlorine clinging to them as he rose from the water, pulling himself out fluidly without even bothering to use the steps. The weight of the water pulled down into his swim trunks and he made a face, hating how they hung around his legs and felt so much heavier once he was out of the water. Yet he didn't mind how they clung to his ass and balls, no, even the faint outline of his sheath discernible through the otherwise modest fabric.

Shane blinked at him, still damp after having spent some time drying off under the full-body fur drier, which was at the side of the swimming pool. There were a few others left in there, just a couple of swimmers doing laps at such a later hour, and they knew, from experience, that they would not be bothered.

Smirking faintly, the coyote turned with a flick of his tail, sweeping it over the back of his legs and exposing his rump – but only for a moment. Kody was well-used to his teasing play by that point, following him closely, knowing that he would get to see more, if only he played the little game that Shane so enjoyed.

A little game here, a little flirt there, the dance back and forth that got them both hot and horny, the tip of Kody's cock poking out of his sheath even then, desperate to make itself known. But it was only when he followed Shane all the way back into the deserted locker room he took the lead and advantage of the moment, pinning the coyote up against the metal lockers between his arms.

"Mmmm…"

Kody let out a low, grumbling growl, his lips twitching along the line of his teeth. As a fox, it was hard for him to not look like he was smirking, as if he was forever amused with wicked enjoyment of what was going on. It was all worth it to see just how the coyote melted against him, his bare chest shuddering as his breath hitched, struggling merely to breathe normally. If that much had not been enough to tell Kody just how Shane was feeling, the bulge rising sharply in the coyote's mostly dry trunks told the tale.

They probably weren't going to make it to the showers that evening – not before they had to make good their exit, that was.

"And I thought you were going to leave without our little ritual," Kody murmured, gently pinning the wet coyote up against the lockers. "That would have really been a shame…"

Shane groaned, the coyote's ears flicking, splaying softly. The fox smirked, though the line of his black lips mostly hid it, the thick brush of his tail still sodden with water, dripping to the locker room floor. It would not stop him, however, not in the slightest.

"I… Ah…" Shane murmured, struggling for breath, his eyes half-lidded and temptingly downcast. "I wanted to see if you'd chase me."

Kody chuckled throatily, his voice dropping another octave, low and husky. Damn, that coyote really got him going… Sometimes, seemingly, without doing anything special at all.

One day, he would work out exactly what that meant. But not that night. No… That night was all about pleasure, Kody growling lustfully and dropping to his knees, completely ignoring the pang of pain that shot through them as he dropped with a little too much force. The ground always seemed closer when he was in a rush, but he pushed the notion aside, yanking Shane's trunks down and exposing the hard length of his swiftly growing shaft.

"Jim and…ah…Si…Simon…" Shane moaned, though he was not in possession of his full capabilities as Kody lapped teasingly over the head of his shaft, savouring the musky glint of pre-cum there as he hardened up fully. "They're still out there…"

"Then you'll have to be quiet," Kody laughed softly. "And quick…"

He didn't think twice as he engulfed the coyote's cock within his maw: an act that he had done many times over. Maybe even a hundred times, though that seemed a little too far, in all honesty, as if he was thinking more of himself and all the lust they had bantered back and forth between them, role swapping sometimes and switching but leaving it all mostly with Kody on top. It was a lightly dominant position, but the fox had mentioned once to the coyote just how he longed to snap his jaws shut – not hard enough to really do any damage, of course – around the creamy fur of his throat. Biting in the claim of fucking… Now, that really was hot.

If how Shane had shivered and cum even harder than usual when Kody had revealed that little fantasy to him was any indicator of how he felt about it too, it may well be something that they got to explore one day, together.

That night, however, Kody swallowed down the coyote's cock as if he had forgotten to lust for anything else, taking the tapered tip expertly into the back of his throat. He may well have been down on his knees though the fox did not by any means feel it was a submissive position for him to take: not when he was the one who held all the cards in his paw.

He knew exactly how he felt about it too, tonguing Shane's cock and relishing in the coyote's moans, just how easy it was to control him. There was a true sense of power to be had in pleasing another with a blowjob, even if Kody had no intention of letting the coyote cum until he had had his pleasure.

Quickly though… There was only so much time. They had played in the locker rooms before, as well as the showers and out in the car park, around the back of the building, yet not getting caught was imperative. The risk of it all tickled the back of Kody's mind, stimulating something that merely fucking a partner in the privacy of a bedroom or some other private space just couldn't match up to. Thankfully, Shane had similar leanings, risking it all for the sake of kinky fun with an element of concern that, maybe, just maybe, they were going to get caught.

So, they could enjoy their time together, Shane grunting, clamping a paw around his own muzzle just to keep himself a little quieter. Kody groaned around the coyote's cock, using every wicked trick at his disposal to rile Shane up more and more. The wagging, sweeping brush of the coyote's tail gave away even more than his words could.

Kody pressed on, working him up, the bitter taste of pre-cum teasing onto the back of his tongue, lust rising. The fox had not thought it was possible to be harder and needier than he was at that moment, yet Shane seemed to get him wound up to incredible lengths every time they came together.

Yes… Yes, there was something between them, something they would enjoy in depth as their relationship progressed. Sometimes the best relationships had the most unconventional beginnings.

It would not, most likely, be the kind of story they told in public, however.

Kody was too tempted to drag everything out a little longer, despite the rush, the biting need and the chasing urge. He had caught his prey and, now, he wanted more, that blistering peak of climax surging within him. Yet he lapped down the length of the coyote's cock, swirling his tongue around the tapered tip that was so familiar to his own. Kody had a bigger knot than Shane, which the coyote had already had once, when they had fucked in a private changing room, staying tied together for twenty heart pounding minutes before they could part again.

That still was one of Kody's favourite memories of him. In the future, there would be many more favourite memories.

He leaned into the moment, letting himself savour the seconds as he moaned, all those tiny vibrations travelling down the full length of Shane's shaft into his lower abdomen. The coyote whimpered, turning his cheek side-on to the metal lockers, the metal rattling lightly behind him as he shifted his weight.

"Ah... Fuck... Kody..."

Kody didn't stop, working him up more and more, that length hard and throbbing within the tight seal of his lips. Even the knot began to swell, pumping up seemingly with every downward stroke of his muzzle down his cock, tongue cradling the underside as he fluttered the flexible appendage against the smooth, slick girth.

Yet the fox didn't want him to get off in his muzzle, no, even though that would have contained every drop of cum and mess. It was a neat way to wrap up a quickie, though Kody had other things in mind, sliding back slowly and licking off his lips with a wickedly salacious grin.

"My, oh, my..." He all put purred, his fingers encircling the base of Shane's cock, though the swelling knot made that more difficult with every panted breath and passing moment. "You are needy today. You should have called me, if you wanted to get your rocks off this much."

"Mmph, fucking tease," Shane muttered, no longer as cool or as collected as he usually was, his tail wagging faintly. "Your number rubbed off my paw though, forgot when I washed up. You'll have to give it to me again."

Ah, just another part of the game, yet a game that they both loved.

But it was a game they could play out, together, in any way they willed, Shane growling softly and more obligingly turning to face the lockers. His palms tried to come down flat against the metal, but Kody wasn't about to have that as the fox pinned him wickedly to it, tugging down his trunks to show off his cock. The hard member sprang out, the tip a little narrower than the coyote's, though the pre-cum that had been lightly beading there smeared across the head. Most of it, however, had been rubbed away by his still wet trunks.

It didn't matter, as long as he took it slowly. As long as he took a breath and paused for a moment, pressing his cock up under Shane's tail, seeking that tight pucker of his tail hole. Shane grunted, wagging his tail, and the fox would have grabbed it, his fingers encircling the root of it, if the chance had been there.

That was okay. Maybe another time. Shane moaned as Kody pressed into him, the long, slow slide of his cock punctuated by his hips drawing back a touch, just to thrust with a little more force. He had to, after all, penetrate his partner duly, and he could not be too gentle when it came to that, every nerve ending on fire, the need to cum, to fuck, overpowering.

"Mmmm…"

Yet Kody needed to control it, panting heavily, rolling his shoulders back, his paws coming down on either side of Shane's head. The coyote bowed his muzzle submissively, arching his back to roll his backside right back on to the fox's cock, showing him, very clearly, what he wanted. Even words in that moment seemed too sacred to be spoken, whimpering softly, breathy moans shared between them with throaty grunts. When the full length of his dick was driven all the way up to the hilt inside the coyote, Kody thrust in earnest, testing out Shane's readiness with deep strokes of his cock.

It was all he needed, grunting, moaning, licking his lips, still trying to be as quiet as possible. Oh, they knew the risks they were taking, but there was still only so much they could do, especially when such heated lust curled around them. It was quite like a form of magic, though not one that either could wield without the other, driving the needy pound of the fox's hips while the coyote could not help himself from grinding back.

Passion and lust… Truly, they were things that needed one another to be shown in their full might. Shane rasped out a groan, shoulders shuddering, and Kody pressed his muzzle over the coyote's shoulder, resting his chin there and wagging his tail faintly.

"Unff… Tell me…if I need to go slower, or anything…"

"No…" Shane managed to force out, a high-pitched whine clawing at his throat. "More… Harder…"

That was something the fox was very keen to oblige, his paw closed around the coyote's cock as he jerked him off. It may have been a moment shared between them, yet it was still raw and lustful, savaged with ragged breaths, grunts and moans. The slide of his cock into the coyote's delectably tight hole poured into Kody like water, filled up from the toes and higher still through his entire body. Kody huffed, hunching his shoulders as he curled his fingers and dug his short claws into the waterproof tiles of the locker rooms.

Shane whined and Kody pressed the full length of his body, as much as he was able, against the coyote, letting him climax. It pulled through the coyote as he bucked and groaned, a strangled gasp breaking his lips as if he was not truly in control of his body. Yet he didn't need to be, not when Kody was there to hold him, to be there for him, to do everything needed in supporting him through every pulse and erratic throb of orgasm. Spurts of cum shot from his cock, each one painting the lockers, for there was no space between him and the metal, just enough for his shaft not to bash into them.

"Oh, ohhhhh..."

Shane trembled, tail dropping a little, yet their fuck was not finished yet, their ears pricked just in case anyone had heard something and was coming to investigate. Thankfully for them, they were still undiscovered in there and had nothing to worry about, even though they were risking it all when they should have perhaps just gone to one of their homes to do what they ached for so dearly. Yet it was that risk that bonded them and brought them together in a way that, otherwise, would not have been possible.

So, they needed that moment: one last fuck of chiselled, defined bodies coming together. The coyote had a bit of softness around his stomach and, almost tenderly, the fox slid his paw up over it, letting his fingers dig in ever so slightly. He thrust and thrust, the knot of his cock swelling – but, that time, he had to keep his full knot out of the coyote's backside. That would have been a recipe for disaster, as alluring as it would have been simultaneously.

But they could make it work, thrust after thrust bringing the fox over the edge, clamping his jaws shut as his tail stiffened and he filled Shane's backside. His tight hole clenched with a sultry squeeze around him, Shane still aware enough to pull out a trick or two just to drive Kody crazy. His seed was contained, however, taken up by the slutty coyote's ass: a fox in control and on top for once. That had always been the position that had brought the most pleasure to Kody and, well, he wanted to explore even more of it with Shane.

Even if he wouldn't be averse to role swapping and trying out, well, pretty much everything with the coyote.

He leaned up against the coyote, grunting softly, relishing in the sensation of that lean, hard muscle, how Shane pushed back against him with a subtle whimper. They wouldn't be able to stay there for very long, but they had enough time with each other, just enough, relaxing in the afterglow, their legs quivering.

His fur dried slowly, trunks still clinging to his backside. Kody drew in a shuddering breath, chest catching as his heart, much to his surprise, seemed to skip a beat.

The next time Kody and Shane came together would be in Shane's living room, after good food and even better wine. But the pair would always remember their start, sneaking around the locker rooms and sneaking less than hidden glances at each other's bodies.

When their beginning was so alluring, who would have ever wanted to forget it?

Full Access Gym

Max smirked as he leaned over the reception desk at the gym, which was set in an old industrial unit. It meant it was a little on the cold side in winter – and a little on the warm side in summer – but the snow leopard was more than okay with that. He was used to adapting to conditions around him and, frankly, it was just something he was used to by that point.

"Aw, George," he wheedled, his long, fluffy tail swishing back and forth, like he wasn't in the middle of doing something that he'd done a good many times before already. "I know you don't want me to leave the gym, you know I know…"

It was all part of their little game, though, really, Max shouldn't have been getting his time there for free as the big donkey shook his head, frowning a little.

"What – again? Max…"

He clicked his tongue against the roof of his mouth, making a soft clucking noise, though it came through more with an air of disappointment than anything else. The snow leopard hesitated, but only for a moment. He had to trust things, after all. Besides, George had fucked him in the back of his truck the other week, so things had to be good between them, even growing closer, kinda.

At least, that was what Max hoped was happening. He rather liked the donkey and had done so since he had stepped into the gym, the big, burly jack catching his attention instantly. The gym was set up with a cool modern vibe in shades of grey and blue with plenty of equipment but also big, open spaces for floor and mat work: crossfit, heavy lifting and the like. Yet it was George who had caught his attention right off the bat with his tall, upright ears, his bristling brown fur that looked a little rough but, in all honesty, was often ruffled across his upper back and around his wrists where he placed the barbell and used lifting straps.

Max was sure that the thick hair could be smoothed back down again if that was what the donkey wanted, but it just added to his charm.

The donkey's muzzle was a softer grey where the hair was finer, allowing the dark skin beneath to show through, his nostrils soft and velvety – though not as much so as his lips. Max should know that, for the feline had spent more than enough time kissing them, bowed and bent under the donkey's body like he was a weight to be lifted, nothing more than a tool that could be shifted to the donkey's will.

Of course, the jack was ripped, even if his thick coat hid a lot of it, softening hard definition across his chest and even down his stomach and across his abdominal muscles. His six-pack was there, however, most definitely, and George had confessed once to him that it sometimes put him off working out for physical appearance when he would have had to trim his coat all the way down just to see it. There were a lot of fluffier anthros in the world too who had similar issues. Even Max's thick fur coat made him look softer and cuddlier, especially in winter, despite him using the gym at least five days a week.

That was how things had started, kind of. He hadn't been able to pay for his gym membership for the following month and tried his luck on with George, wanting to see if there was some way that the two of them could come to an arrangement.

Max had a lot going for him too and he knew he could push things the moment he caught the donkey's eyes on him. There was nothing quite like a long, fluffy tail to draw the eye, after all, and the snow leopard had more than a few tricks up his sleeve, swishing it back and forth just so the motion would catch George's eye more and more. When he had sprawled over the top of the reception desk, he'd half expected to be kicked out and shown the door, though the donkey had been receptive.

Rather invitingly so…

Thus, the deal had been struck, flirting back and forth, Max exchanging sexual favours to keep coming to the gym and using it as he pleased. Of course, things wouldn't have been that easy if the snow leopard had not been as respectful of the gym and equipment as he was, though Max made sure he stayed in George's good books. The donkey, after all, was not someone he wanted to piss off. He appreciated very much everything that George did for him, for the donkey did not have to allow him to use the gym for free, keeping his membership going.

There was something there, something crackling and simmering – and that was why the snow leopard pushed things a little further that evening. It was late, too late for anyone to be there besides them, and Max had already dragged George out of the back room to chat, as the donkey had been doing paperwork.

Paperwork wouldn't keep the big cat from getting what he wanted from the donkey: it never had.

"Yeah, so…" Max grinned, cocking his head a little more. "You… Well, I was thinking, I could give you another favour and…figured you may be up for going out with me sometime?"

Oh, it was forward – though that was exactly what Max had been going for. Sure, he'd been dancing around things for ages already, flirting back and forth with George, curious to see just how far he could push things, yet…it had to change. Whether that meant that he coughed up the cash to pay for his membership and things carried on as if nothing had happened or they took the next step together. The two anthros didn't have to follow any route or pattern, no – but they had to do something, for carrying on as they were most likely wasn't going to work long-term.

Sometimes a guy just had to shoot his shot and that was all Max could hope for: a soft landing.

The donkey pulled back a little, blinking at him while his thick, ropey tail swung behind him.

"Sorry, cat, must have misheard you there," he said, more suave than Max had given him credit for, leaning forward over the desk. "I think you said that you want to take me out somewhere?"

Max grinned, his smile a little shakier than he would have liked. He'd just have to deal with it though.

"Uh… Yeah. I know what you're into in here," he said, his tone heavily laden with the implications of what they had done in the gym, together. "But… I don't know anything about you outside the gym. So, what do you say?"

George grinned and shook his head, though the donkey held back his smile slightly as if he was trying not to allow it to pull at his lips too much.

"Is that right?" He said boldly, crossing his arms across his chest. "And you can't pay your membership this month?"

"No…" The feline dragged out the word, whiskers quivering. "But…I can get coffee?"

Maybe he really should have come clean that it was all a game, that they were just playing back and forth and seeing where things went – all while getting something out of the deal, of course, that benefited them both. Yet Max didn't know how much of the whole thing was George willingly believing that he couldn't pay or if the donkey understood the full score.

Max had always been able to pay, but…he'd just started the game when he saw his chance. Was that so wrong? The feline sure hoped not, but he could never be sure how something would play out. That was part of the fun of it all.

He'd come clean about that. Yet George was looking at him with that special little twinkle in his eye Max had hoped was reserved especially for him, though he could not be certain. He could only hope and want, for the fluttering of something more had long ago risen in his chest, taking root behind his ribcage.

It would be well-protected there, but never against the threat of his heart being broken.

Until then, he would have to work with what he had, going forward, step by step.

"So… You can't pay your membership, huh?"

Max blinked. Oh, so it seemed George was back in the game. What did that mean for him?

The cat tried to go along with it, sliding back and attempting to look meek and a little pathetic. The trick had been working well for him so far, so it couldn't hurt to play along a little more, even then.

"No…" He mewled, whiskers quivering as he held back a chuckle. "No… But I can do something else for you, if you renew my membership for another month?"

"Mm…" George's eyes slid towards the main door to the gym; the only other door in there, which could be easily opened from the inside, was a fire escape door. "You locked the door?"

Max smirked.

"Already put in the code on the pin pad, mate."

George didn't answer, the donkey instead practically stalking, as if he had become a predator himself in that moment, around the desk with his chin tipped cockily high. He didn't need to do much to appear bigger and more imposing than Max as the feline's heart pounded harder and faster, his glutes clenching against a monster that he was sure would soon be driven up inside him.

Indeed, the donkey's long shorts, loose and comfortable, were already tented out with that beast of a cock, swollen and thick, clearly already bursting from the donkey's sheath. Against himself, even though he had intended to play the game for a little longer, he shivered, letting out the softest of yowls.

George smirked.

"Sometimes I think my dick is the only reason you keep on coming back here, again and again, cat," he teased, though Max knew that the situation there was very different to how the donkey put it. "You want this inside you, ramming deep... But you never quite know how to get what you want, do you?"

"Mmmph..."

The feline shook his head, barely even knowing what he was saying. It was so easy to let George lead, to take control, though Max never wanted to be a passive player in their fun either, oh no.

Yet he wanted so sorely to see where the donkey was going to take him that time.

"Well, you know what my mouth and my under tail can do, don't you?" Max managed to shoot back in a few moments, his voice lighter and breathier than usual. "I don't... Mmm!"

The donkey's enormous paw (or hand, depending on the individual's preference – didn't really matter) came out, complete with the chunky, hoof-like fingertips that spread out at the tips: neither claws nor nails like some anthros had. Yet that was not the matter at all as he cupped Max's crotch and rolled the heel of his paw down to the fingers over the feline's cock and balls, teasing him as he swelled. Unlike the donkey, the cat did not have a sheath that needed to free his erection – which only made it easier for George to access when the two of them spent time together.

Even though Max had said nothing, he hadn't slept with anyone else since the second month of them hooking up. And the hook ups had grown increasingly frequent since then, not only at the end of the month when the next month's gym payment was due.

I hope this goes well…

And Max didn't just mean sex, of course. No… It was something much more than that, something that he wanted very badly to get into. Even as George drew him roughly up against his body, a large arm around him to crush the smaller feline to his chest. The donkey was easily a good head and shoulders taller than him, though he was a larger species, and the snow leopard could only mewl helplessly as he succumbed.

He really would have done anything for George, whether he was getting something in return for it or not. Just because.

The donkey's tongue invaded his mouth, hot and probing, casually dominant, as if George already knew exactly what it was that he could take from his partner of the moment. Even though neither knew where things were to go, Max melted against him, letting the donkey do as he willed, savouring the shape of the anthro pressed up against him. However, it was more as if he was the one melding to George's shape than the other way around, his long tail lashing back and forth wantonly, obviously betraying his need.

It was not as if the feline would have wanted to hold back or hide it away in any way, after all. He was there, that night, to lay it all bare and see where things fell, though being bent backwards just so the donkey could get at his lips, dominating his muzzle, still made him feel small and as if he could be swept away with whatever George needed or craved from him that time.

"Mmph!"

Stumbling backwards, Max flicked his tail, his hard-on evident as George sat him down on a padded bench in the dumbbell area. There were three set up there, though they had mostly stuck to places around the gym like behind the reception, in the back rooms, in the showers, the locker rooms: typical things like that. The benches were new and the feline yowled as that large paw caressed his crotch all over again, rubbing and massaging, manipulating his shaft as he swelled eagerly into the donkey's touch.

"You just come here for this, don't you?"

Max shook his head, mewling softly. But he couldn't call the words that he wanted so badly to his lips, to tell George that, no, there was something more. At least it was not what the donkey actually believed and still was all part of their game.

That much, he could deal with. And make sure, at the very least, George knew the truth at the end of it all...

"Mmmmph... No..." He tried, grunting breathlessly, the donkey tugging at his jogging bottoms to get them down his hips and over his erection. "Want...you..."

He meant that as much, much more than George's body, of course, but could not know how the jack took it. It didn't matter, however, as the snow leopard freed his own dick, springing forth with nothing to contain it, his heavy, white-furred balls dropping below. It was strange to sit on the workout bench with nothing on his lower half, though he didn't get a chance to appreciate the cool of the bench on his ass as George took his arms and forced him out of his T-shirt too.

"When am I going to get to see you too then?" Max said, calling a bit of his flirtatious nature back, catching his breath. "I don't think you want me to just be sitting here all pretty like now, do you?"

The donkey grinned and merely tugged down his shorts. He didn't bother pulling them lower than his thick sheath, letting the monster of his grey shaft, with a few pink flecks on the rear side of the fleshy head, flop out. It hung down under its own weight, though swiftly swelled to full hardness, bobbing and twitching right into the cat's paws. Max whimpered, looking up at the donkey, though he was already at the right height, sitting on the bench with George right there in front of him, to do everything the donkey wanted of him at that time.

"You know what to do…"

Oh, and Max surely did. He parted his lips, kissing the thick, flat tip with sloppy adoration, his tongue sweeping around it lusciously, familiar with the shape of the donkey's dick. Although his tongue was a little on the rougher side, being a feline, it was not harsh enough on the donkey's cock, of course, to cause him any harm, though it offered additional stimulation. More even than the wide, fleshy expanse of the donkey's tongue on his shaft, though they did not often swap roles. When it came to domination and submission, they were two anthros who knew very surely what they liked.

And that was okay too. For it allowed Max to take what he needed while devoutly giving George everything he yearned for too. In sex, it was the perfect balance, though neither would have been averse at all to trying other things too; they just needed a little more trust between them, playing back and forth and learning about one another. That was exactly why Max wanted to be with the donkey more, to learn more, to do more – to see just where things could go.

He couldn't think of that right then, however, locking into the moment, revelling in the soft, spongy sensation of the jack's cock pressing over his lips. He moaned around it as he kissed it deeply, parting his jaws wider and wider and wider to take it inside. Fuck, that was hot, the mammoth size of the donkey's cock putting him in a state of awe every time. Why, even the feline's fluffy tail curled around him, as if he was trying to comfort himself, to tell himself that he was able to do it, that he could please George just as he wanted.

Of course, his maw was good enough, his tongue cradling the thick meat as it pushed urgently into his mouth. It must have been some time since George last got off and Max was more than willing to help him out there, using his paws to rub and tease the donkey's sheath, pressing down hard enough to stimulate the inside. If he had more time, he would have dipped his fingers inside, letting the donkey grunt and stomp until he grabbed him and fucked his face hard enough to leave bruises on his lips the next day.

Fuck, Max loved when he did that... Yet it was not to be that night, not as he gave George a sloppy, lewd blowjob, swallowing hard and repeatedly to take his cock down into the back of his throat. He had to keep going, had to have the full length, even though the thick bulge was evident in his throat, making his heart hammer and pound. It was too big for him, really, but he wouldn't allow himself to miss out on the chance to savour that hot length filling his mouth.

No... Not when it came to pleasing George. With the donkey, his pleasure was all that mattered. And it had been that way for a long time indeed, even though George always made sure, even though he had never had to, that the snow leopard had his pleasure taken care of too, even aftercare.

Maybe that was why he'd started falling for George, even if only a little. Just how he was made Max want to dig a little deeper.

Yet the girth of his cock laying across the snow leopard's tongue had him gulping and groaning, swapping the roles of predator and prey in a moment so heady that it should have been practically illegal. The donkey thrust, rolling his hips, his glutes deliciously tight as Max grabbed them, digging his short claws in to rile the jack up even more. He knew just how that got George going.

"Unff… Can never do anything lightly, unff…can you?"

Max didn't mind that. Not one little bit as he let his eyes close halfway and moaned like a whore around the donkey's cock, letting him hold the back of his head and thrust and *thrust*. He could tap out at any point if George was being too rough with him, though, honestly, Max didn't think that could happen. Something would have to go seriously wrong to make him want to stop or slow down – so he languished there in the slide of that glorious dick and the fat, plump head gliding over his tongue.

It crammed into the back of his mouth and down his throat as if it belonged there, every thrust making Max's cock throb more and more. The snow leopard was not going to last long if he was going to be treated like that; however, it was the donkey who had been holding back for too long already.

Max shuddered in place, doing his best just to keep his head still and the angle tilted a little, all so George could better slide down his throat, claiming every inch for his own. The donkey hammered in, a thumb briefly rubbing behind the cat's ear; a small touch Max did not ignore. He hoped it meant what he thought it did, though he could not be sure.

What he could be sure of, however, was the donkey's need as he let out those adorable little grunts and shifted his weight, stomping heavily. His shorts slid a little lower, exposing his nuts, though Max was, in part, responsible for that while the jack was distracted. Who was he to deny himself a good squeeze and tease of such a fine ass?

And there were multiple meanings of that word…as he was keen to remind George of!

He chuckled throatily around the donkey's dick even as his face was fucked, though the snow leopard was very much not the one in control. He did not need to be, not as George hammered in harder and faster, giving him the ride that he had so sorely needed. The feline's eyes watered and he yowled, however muffled the sound was, as the donkey hammered in, crushing his nose into the thicker ruff of hair around his crotch.

Yet that was what Max craved, moaning deeply as George finally lost control, ejaculating into his mouth. It was rough and it was crude. It had to be lewd, for that was all it needed to be, the cock head throbbing thickly, swelling within Max's mouth as the feline tongued it needily. Every rope of cum splattered into his mouth and hit the back of his throat, though the cat did his best not to choke on it – solely for the fact it would have interrupted their fun.

And he didn't want that, not as he let the thick swill of cum swirl around his mouth, under his tongue and around his teeth. He moaned, gulping as much as he could, though he was not averse to cum dribbling out from the corners of his lips too. It didn't matter if it mussed up his muzzle, drying into his fur and marking his neck and chest: only that they got what they wanted.

Time was ticking, however, and he was barely with himself as that meat dragged back from his muzzle, pulling over his tongue even as the feline tried to flick his tongue up against the still engorged head. Yet the donkey did not soften in the slightest as he pulled back, letting his cock pop free of the cat's lips. The head remained flared, though perhaps not to its fullest extent, even though that had never been a problem for them in the past.

"Get on the bench, kitty."

Max blinked up at him. What did George mean? He was too far gone, lost in his own lust and adoration for the donkey who he still had to confess to. Thankfully for him, there was a strong paw on his shoulder, turning him around and guiding him down, belly first on to the bench.

"This okay with you, cat?"

He loved how George checked in with him too, even though he would have spoken up if anything was wrong. They'd set safe words and parameters early on, so they knew just how far they could go.

"Yeah… Unff… Yeah…"

It was all Max could say as he flipped his tail up out of the way, listening to the tantalising rustle of clothes as the donkey disrobed behind him. Hm…

And then the donkey was pressed against him with the monster of his dick grinding over his rump, smearing pre-cum into the cat's fur. Max simply didn't have it in himself to care, panting heavily, trying to wiggle his tail a little further out of the way still, for the donkey was going to have him one way or another. He just had to take it with a low groan, letting his buttocks and hind end relax as much as possible, not even having to rock back on to George's shaft.

George knew what he liked by then anyway, driving into him long and slow, drawing out the moment as if he was trying to make the penetration last forever. Max would have begged for it if he had breath left in his lungs to do so, panting heavily, a soft yowl breaking his lips as if it was a kiss.

"Mmm... Unfff... Yesss..."

He hissed, trying to arch back, his cock trapped between his fur and the bench, though it was soft enough for him not to care. As long as he had George there to cover him, to lay his powerful, broad body over him, to take him as he needed to be taken.

Only the donkey had ever been able to make his blood sing quite like that. Just another little reason why the snow leopard had fallen for him as he had.

"Mmmph..." Max moaned. "Please..."

"Mmm, anything for you."

Fuck, that was hot. Max sure hoped the donkey meant it, for he may well have said the same to him too.

He wanted to give the donkey everything he could, the best he could. They just had to find the chance for it, together.

In the moment, however, it was all about the rhythm, the deep stretch under his tail taking his breath away, lips parted, the hint of a smile around them. Max moaned deeply, pressing his muzzle down as submissively as he could into the bench, though need trembled deeply through his midsection, all the way down into his loins. He grunted and twisted, yet George was right there to take him, leaning over him, bearing down lightly on his hips with just the right amount of pressure to keep him in place. No more and most certainly no less.

I can't wait to take him out for that coffee...or dinner...or something...anything...

Anything would do as the donkey thrust him to orgasm. It was not exactly paws-free when his cock was grinding into the bench with such force, but it was more than enough. He howled, struggling not to claw at it and rip it up, for that was something George would have most definitely not been happy about. It was worth it all to quiver there, poised as if frozen in orgasm, painting the bench in his cream. Thankfully for the feline, most of it was soaked back up by the fur of his belly and crotch, however sticky and uncomfortable that ended up being.

His tail hole tightened, squeezing around the donkey's cock, doing his very best to coax him closer and closer to the edge. To Max's back, the donkey grunted and the cat could almost feel his lips wobbling, thrusts growing a little more erratic as he sped up and up, the swing and bounce of his nuts off the feline's running rampant.

"Unff… Just…a little… Mmmmph… Fuuuuuck!"

It was not quite the point of orgasm for George but it was close enough, just a few thrusts more bringing him over the edge for a second time, showing off his sexual prowess to the feline in all its glory. He brayed out his release, leaning forward and hunching over the snow leopard, as if he wanted to be as close as possible.

The moment was right and he settled into it, pillowing his head on his arms as release rolled through him. It was better than his own, to feel the donkey letting loose inside him, long, hot spurts of virile cum splattering into his rump, filling him up to the brim with cream. Not all of it could fit inside, forced back out in a squelching, wet mess of seed along the length of the jack's cock, though that could all be cleaned up in due course.

They were just there to enjoy the moment, the carnal outpouring of need that was so very sorely desired. The two of them had just had to find a way to bring it through for them, in a way that was just, well…them…

They could never have followed someone else's lead, after all.

"Mmmm…"

As George dipped his head to nuzzle at the back of the snow leopard's shoulders, Max glanced back. He really should say something about the gym membership stuff, he didn't want George to get the wrong idea or think he was screwing him around. He wanted everything…well…to be a clean slate. Yet it was hard to find the words or even to talk with a thick prick straining his rump wide around it.

"You know…"

The feline said, his long tail swinging lazily as he looked back at the donkey jack. Yet he dragged out the words as if he was revealing a secret that was only then coming to the forefront of everything. Curious, George drew back a little to see him better, his softening cock tugging at Max's rump. The feline shivered, though didn't help him slide out, leaving the flared tip still tucked inside.

"I didn't need my gym fee covered…" Max growled, licking his lips. "I just wanted to see if you'd keep fucking me. Kinda thought I should let you know about that before, you know, a coffee date or dinner date or something."

The donkey pulled back, popping his cock free, his eyes wide, nostrils flared. For a moment, Max thought he'd gone too far, that he had pushed things too much – but, really, it had been fun then, even if he hadn't thought it would go as far as it did, with him exchanging excellent sex for another month of a gym membership. But the donkey shook his head slowly and let out a long, braying chuckle that, at the very least, settled Max's mind.

Damn… So, he hadn't gone too far then at all. That was something. A very good something, in fact.

Who could have known that full access to the gym, for free, could have led to something more…though Max was more than happy to go along for the ride and experience everything, with George, exactly as it was meant to be.

Some things… They were meant to *be*.

Wet Fur

It was easy to catch the eye of someone in the gym, but, well, it was the kind of establishment that was most certainly for adults only. Everyone who went there knew that and if they didn't know it, well…they found out on the sign-up paperwork and definitely during their first session there too. A gym with a small pool, sauna and steam room attached, it had started as a meeting place for anthros who were guys and wanted to hook up with guys – then gone from strength to strength.

A casual place for weightlifting, cardio, relaxing, having sex and more… What more could anyone ask for? Of course, it wasn't the kind of place for everyone: and it was never intended to be.

That was just why Mike went to the gym, however, the chocolate Labrador's tail practically always wagging. Sometimes his tail got tired, but, well…that was just something he was happy to deal with. He'd much rather be cheerful and smiling than feeling down in the dumps, though that didn't mean the dog anthro didn't have his own needs to be met either.

He took his time in the gym, where everyone could work out in whatever clothes, within mild reason, they were the most comfortable with. It meant that most in the weightlifting and cardio areas would strip down to just shorts and a shirt, though some wore tighter, supportive underwear to exercise in. Cleaning wipes, towels and other necessities were, of course, provided so that shed fur and sweat could be cleaned up from equipment after its use. Anyone who didn't look after the gym and the facilities provided for them wouldn't last very long there, which suited Mike just fine.

He relaxed in the machine area, switching off a little while he took his body through the motions, grunting as he pressed the weight up on the angled leg press. His quads burned and he brought the weight all the way down, as close to his body with his legs bent, as he could get, so that it caught his glutes too. Nothing was wasted, after all, when he was working out and he didn't want to skip a workout just because his dick was plumping out his sheath even then.

"Mmph…"

Mike hadn't really headed into the gym that day, after all, because he wanted to work out. Sure, that was all part of it, but he really wanted to head back to the relaxation areas and the pool. Maybe even the loungers set up by the pool, though there was rarely a lot of lounging going on there… Sure, giving head in the steam room had been hot when he had first got into the scene there, but the humidity of having steam wafting around him, as good as it was for his body, made it something he put aside quite swiftly. Better to enjoy the view of others taking slow, lustful pleasure in there, rather than offer his services.

At least, that was Mike's opinion. And he didn't have to push any boundaries of his own that he didn't want to as he relaxed there, going through his leg routine, from the leg press to the leg extension and the leg curl. There was a good new calf raise machine too that had him hissing with how effective it was, though the Labrador appreciated not having to swap to the barbells or dumbbells to get in a quick, effective leg workout. Sure, compound lifts would have done better, technically, but using the machines meant he didn't all that much have to use his brain.

That was really the kind of day that Mike needed to shut off his brain – and he was going to, most certainly. The dog trotted through to the showers at a light jog, eagerness in his step, the very moment he'd finished his exercise and wiped down the equipment, waving to a golden eagle anthro who had a particularly broad, well-defined chest.

"Hey, Mack!"

"Hey, Mike, looking good!"

Mike smiled. Compliments were handed out freely there: just another thing for him to like about the place. It was so easy to be himself and maybe that was something everyone there should really have been thinking about taking forward into the real world too. It was not all a light, safe environment like that one.

He only had to shower off and get his fur all wet to clean himself for the pool. It was not particularly big, but the canine's ears pricked the moment he stepped through, a long glass window looking out on the outside exercise area, even though it was dark at the moment, in the early evening. The nights had started drawing in earlier than Mike had realised, though he always had somewhere to go to make sure he was comfortable in the longer dark of the Autumn and Winter.

"Mmm…"

He paused before getting in the pool, enjoying the view of an Alaskan Malamute canine, thicker and fluffier than a husky, bent over one of the loungers with his tail in the air. It didn't look like the most comfortable of positions, but that didn't matter to the dragon fucking him, a long, green tail undulating lustfully as he filled the Malamute's tail hole. Even though Mike didn't know either of their names, he wouldn't have at all minded joining in on their fun if the opportunity arose.

Yet someone already seemed to have their eye on him, even if Mike only realised when the ripples lapping at his body in the water, chest deep, gained more form and purpose as they were pushed away from an incoming body. That was just the way things went there, the unexpected happening purely because an offer was made – and accepted of course. Non-consensual sex or trying to persuade anyone who didn't want to fuck was very much not accepted there. In the early days, a few had been thrown out, though they didn't appear to have all that much trouble after that point.

Which was a good thing as Mike found himself backed up pleasantly to the side of the pool, his ears pricked and his pink tongue lolling out already.

"Hey…" The African Wild Dog, with striking markings in brown, black and white, greeted him with his tongue hanging out, though it was suave and teasing, a glint in his eye. "Name's Strike. I've seen you around though…"

"Mike," the dog said, licking his lips. "Yeah, I'm Mike."

He wished he said something better than that, that he was clearer in his attentions, yet the rise in his swim trunks, a tighter fit without being swim briefs, told the tale for him. That was something, indeed, that the canine could always rely on and not even the cool lap of the pool against him was enough to settle down his carnal needs.

The African wild dog came in a little closer, his pink tongue, once more, sweeping along the outside of his muzzle. The next thing Mike knew was the other anthro's paw cupping his balls and sheath, a thumb just about brushing up against the base of his cock where it was protruding from his sheath.

"Unff…"

Mike panted heavily, eyes half-lidded, putty in the gorgeous wild dog's paws already. But that was the way he liked it, even though he thought he was just going to enjoy the view for a little before getting into it.

"Come up here," Strike suggested, a smirk on his lips that quirked them up on one side. "Up on the side… I'll see that you get what you want."

Mike followed the line of his gaze. Huh… So, the Wild Dog wanted him to sit up there? That was interesting… But he didn't mind it at all, drawing himself out of the pool with his forearms and a grunt of effort. The weight of gravity closed down around him as the Labrador groaned, his fur soaked through, even his swim trunks pulling down a little with the weight of the water soaking them through. It was always a strange shift to get out of the pool, when weightlessness had always been a deeply rooted sense before.

But it was easy not to worry about that or let it linger in his mind in the slightest as he sat there, legs dangling in the water, and the African wild dog took over. Strike smirked as he came in closer, pinging the dog's trunks down smoothly to free the spring of his erection. The hard, red rocket of dog meat throbbed wantonly, a bead of pre-cum faintly glistening at the tip where it had not yet been washed away.

"Mmm..." Strike groaned, hefting himself up a little more, though the pool was shallow enough there that his muzzle was near the right height for him to do as he willed. "That's good... Heh, good timing, you coming in here..."

Of course, the facilities there would always be thoroughly cleaned, so no one ever had to worry about bodily fluids or anything unhygienic, which was just how Strike could engulf the dog's cock in his mouth right there in the open, swallowing him down. Mike moaned, tongue lolling out, panting heavily as his tongue fluttered and twitched with every breath he dragged into his lungs.

Yet it wasn't enough, not even then, every jot of the dog's attention focused on the wild dog, how his muzzle bobbed and even twisted lightly, his tongue curling and flicking around his meat. Fuck, how did he even move his tongue like that? In getting head, Mike would have thought he was in a position of control and power and yet he felt as if he was the submissive one in. There was a funny amount of power and seduction, after all, that went into giving and receiving head, in allowing a tender, sensitive part of his body to be taken into the jaws of another.

Even though he didn't know Strike personally (he might, from that day on), he had to trust him. There were others around, at least, some fucking on the loungers and even a couple who were fucking in the water, a stag with his legs wrapped around a bear's waist as the bear plunged rampantly into his tail hole, stretching him out. So, he was far from alone there and things were only just heating up with all the lust and attention that went on in there in the evening.

"Mmmph…"

Mike squirmed and tucked his tail down, though it always betrayed him, wagging and wagging, showing off just how into everything he was. Strike moaned around him, letting every soft vibration from his muzzle travel into the Labrador's cock, though his balls were left tucking away within his wet trunks, which was not entirely a comfortable sensation. Still, his sheath pulled back a little more as those seductive, black lips slid down all the way on his cock, caressing and teasing. He trembled, jaw hanging open. How could the wild dog suckle down his cock like that, pressing down tightly with his lips, while his tongue curled and twisted? There didn't seem like there would be enough room in his muzzle for that but, somehow, Strike exceeded even the expectations that Mike didn't know he had.

He was more than willing to go along with everything, however, more of a follower than a leader, though he topped too from time to time.

Okay, so it was pretty rare that Mike topped…but that was his preference. The wild dog slurped on his cock, drawing back to lavish attention on the tip, the trembling, tingling sensations running through his cock forcing Mike to pant when his chest felt too tight. He twitched and shifted his weight, rocking back and forth from one buttock to the other, his head tipping back, even though he wanted to watch every detail, every moment.

Of course, it was the other canine who was in charge there, even the fluff inside his ears damp, some bits with droplets of water clinging to them. The Labrador was struck by a sudden urge to brush those droplets away, yet the action would have proven to be an awful lot more tender than the moment called for. Perhaps it would not have been so bad, however.

There was nothing quite like having a long, hot tongue curling around his cock and lapping up to the tip. It flicked into the slit and he twitched, tensing briefly, yet the overstimulation did not last all that long as he groaned and Strike pulled back, toying with him.

"Come on, pup," he teased, flicking the very tip of his tongue over the head of Mike's cock, drawing him forward as if he was coaxing the Labrador to fall into the water: he angled his torso forward that far, searching out pleasure. "Out of the water, with both of us, properly. I've got what you need right here."

Mike scrambled back as Strike heaved himself fluidly out of the water, fur sodden and water streaming from him. A polar bear glanced over at them and grinned while Strike gently guided the dog to the loungers.

"Mmm…"

The Labrador couldn't help himself from letting out a soft moan and smiled at how Strike's ears twitched, splaying slightly. So, he was not all as suave and as put together as he came off. There was a certain kind of pleasure in watching another anthro unravel themselves in ecstasy.

They'd get there.

Strike sat on the lounger and patted his lap in much a similar fashion to how he had patted the side of the pool to get the Labrador up there originally. The chocolate lab whined and did as he asked, turning his back on the African wild dog, though he rather would have enjoyed getting to see more of him too. He did, however, take just a moment to slip his wet trunks off, all so they didn't get in the way. He noticed, out of the corner of his eye, that Strike did the same.

"Here you go, pup, ride me."

Mike shivered, doing as asked. There was something simply more carnal to putting his back to him, however, so the other canine could position his cock just as he pleased, Mike's own shaft hard and throbbing, dribbling pre-cum now that they were out of the water.

"Mmm..." Mike panted, eyes half-closed, a goofy smile stretching his lips as the wild dog freed his cock, the Labrador straddling his hips with his back to him. "Fuck... Didn't expect someone like you to take me today..."

"What, need a paw on your collar, pup?"

"Unnnff... Ohhhh!"

Mike would have said more to that if not for Strike guiding him down and back onto his cock at that very moment, stretching out his tail hole wonderfully as the African wild dog's cock drove up deep. Gravity pulled Mike down further and further onto his cock, though he was more than relaxed enough to take him, a long, drawn-out groan rising from his lips.

"Ohhhhh..."

"That's it, pup..."

There were eyes on them, though that wasn't anywhere near enough to bring a flush of embarrassment to Mike's cheeks, oh no. He wasn't particularly into being watched, yet there was something gratifying about watching someone else jacking off to the sight of him getting fucked. Mike shuddered, muscles flexing, as he bucked and rode on top of his partner's dick, grinding back, trying to get it to tease over his prostate as much as he could. When he was playing with a partner rather than a toy, however, that often proved difficult. And control was not really in his paws anyway as Strike curled his fingers possessively around Mike's throat, at the front, as if his paw took the place of a collar.

"Unff… Mmmph…"

Mike rode him, hazy with lust, his prick hard and untouched while they were on the lounger. It didn't need to be stroked or caressed in any way, fat, gleaming droplets of pre-cum drooling from his cock with anal stimulation alone. He squeezed, clenching his ass down as hard as he could around Strike's cock, teasing his length. The Wild Dog huffed behind him, grunting in his ear as he half sat up and was then forced to lean back, relaxing along the full length of the lounger with his hind paws kicked out.

"Mmm… You don't know how hot you are…"

But they were both hot, taking advantage of the place and the situation to take what they wanted from each other, the musculature of their bodies defined by the wetness of the fur clinging to them. Mike panted heavily, blood roaring in his ears, but he could not slow the driving, frantic beat of his heart any more than he could halt what was happening. The rising throb of need curled up within him, rising higher and higher, desperate to be seen. As his cock twitched and he bucked frantically on Strike's cock, it had to come out.

And the African wild dog was not far at all behind him, grunting thickly in the back of his throat and tensing as Mike howled out his lust. Dimly, the dog was aware of someone cheering in the pool area, yet he didn't have it in himself to care. Let them look, if they wanted to: he was there to enjoy himself, to luxuriate in every pulse of cum leaping from the tapered tip of his aching prick in splattering ropes. He painted Strike's legs in his seed, marking the lounger, yet both fur and the lounger itself could be cleaned up very easily. His balls ached deeply, the outpouring of lust satisfying, yet not quite enough.

Hopefully there would be another round for them both, though a quickie bragged a delight too as Strike yelped and filled his rump, his paw tightening its grip on Mike's throat, though not enough so that the Labrador could not breathe easily. Mike panted, leaning back, the canine's cock driven up as far into his backside as it was possible to be, even Strike's sheath crinkling back as if it was letting loose a sliver more cock, just for his pleasure.

He trembled as he was filled, those fingers moving on his neck, rolling and massaging.

"Mmmm..." Even Strike's voice was raspier, dropping an octave. "Good, pup..."

Mike whined, his tail wagging, though it was most certainly not against his will. Even then, he swore he could feel the canine's cum sloshing about inside him, filling him, marking him, claiming him. Yet the oozing, drooling drips squelching out of his backside along the line of Strike's cock were more than enough for his overstimulated nervous system to focus on.

With their wet fur grinding against one another, there was surely plenty more time that evening for the chocolate Labrador and the African Wild Dog to get to know one another...

A quickie, after all, was just a warm-up for the main workout!

Sex Between Sets

Aydin growled, his long, striped tail lashing back and forth as the tiger paused between sets. His thighs burned from front squats, where he took the bar across his collarbones, his paws facing away from his body where he curled his fingers around the bar and bent his wrists back. It was a tricky lift to master as it required more flexibility in the wrists and strength there, needing a greater level of skill than simply picking a dumbbell up and setting it down again. Frankly, a lot of the bigger, compound lifts required more focus and practise than many appreciated or realised.

The tiger slipped out of his shirt, ignoring the fact that the fur across his traps was ruffled from doing back squats earlier too, even though he was coming to the end of his workout. The knurling on the barbell tended to pull out little bits of his fur, though scrapes like that were all normal when it came to lifting. Hell, even Aydin had scraped up his shins when doing deadlifts, though he tried not to be too rough on himself as much as he could.

He didn't want to sacrifice his physical fitness and muscle building for temporary appearances, however, not in the slightest. He'd rather build his muscle, to fill out his already round shoulders even more, to see just how he could get his quads to bulge. All muscle, for him, was functional too, of course, for he'd probably never get to where he was trying to lean down and cut fat, more in it to see what he could do. For physical appearances, he could more than do what he wanted in that gym.

Yet Aydin focused on someone else, something else, as he finished his last set, rubbing his wrists, his legs burning. He scratched his lower stomach, letting out a low growl in the nearly deserted gym. There was only one other there and he had been teasing and taunting Aydin for too long.

The okapi, an ungulate with a longer neck than usual and sleek, glossy brown fur – short enough that it was merely hair in a shiny coat – bent over, stretching out a hamstring that was already well stretched out already. His tail was thin and ropey, with a small tuft of hair at the end, his legs striped as if he had zebra heritage. Yet the okapi species, with their longer necks and twisting, flexible tongues, were more akin to giraffes, living in a different terrain and environment.

Aydin growled, tail lashing. Ten at night. No one else was there. That was fine. That was more than fine, that was just as the tiger wanted it to be. For it was high time they settled this "thing" that lay between them.

He knew the okapi. His name was Eli and he had been teasing Aydin for weeks already. He wore tighter and tighter shorts every time Aydin saw him, casting him knowing looks back over his shoulder, smirking and toying with him. It was not as if Aydin could do anything to make a move, besides chatting to Eli, in public, of course, though the feline ached to grope him, to slide his enormous paw over the okapi's nicely round, toned rump.

Eli grinned, swinging his towel back over his shoulder as he strutted by. The okapi was shirtless too, but there was nothing unusual about that, oh no. His shorts, however, barely covered his upper thighs, as if the pockets would have hung out past the legs if they had been the kind of stretchy shorts that had pockets, though Aydin was far too concerned with taking in the okapi with his eyes.

"Mmm…"

"Like what you see, stripes?"

Aydin grunted, a smirk tugging at his lips.

"You think you'd be more careful of my fangs, Eli," he drawled out, standing and rubbing off any lingering sweat from his palms on his bare thighs, shorts falling back into place to the point above his knees. "Considering that you're soft, flexible... I could bend you over my knee right here and do just as I like to you."

Eli grinned, offering Aydin a look at his crotch, the bulge there rising, growing softly. And it was quite a bulge indeed, even if it was not a bulge the tiger had any intention of taking. With just how the okapi had been waving his ass in his face for so long, there was only one thing on Aydin's mind.

"Oooh, showing your fangs? Kinky," Eli laughed, blowing Aydin a kiss. "If you think you've got what it takes, it's quiet enough…now. You can follow me to the showers, if you like. Earn your stripes and all that."

Aydin didn't think Eli fully understood what that saying meant – hell, did it even matter? He was hot on the okapi's heels in a heartbeat of a moment, his heart pounding, breath raking through his windpipe, lungs heaving just to get something near enough air in his lungs. His shoes squeaked as he followed Eli, though he didn't need to go as quickly as he was, trying to close the distance between them.

He already knew where they were going and stripped off his long shorts the moment they stepped into the locker room, dropping them on the ground. His jockstrap swiftly followed, revealing his sheath and balls, a softly barbed cock swiftly making itself known.

Eli had already gone ahead, straight into the communal showers, though there was no one else there. As the hiss of water greeted him, the okapi turning the showers on, he took a moment, rubbing his cock from base to tip and back again.

It was a good cock, though not as smoothly skinned as many would have liked to take up under their tails. The barbs were soft and pliable – reminiscent of what his species would have had many,

many years ago, though pleasure was the name of the game those days, not breeding need. After all, Aydin would never have been interested in breeding.

It was just guys. Guys and only guys. Sure, he played with his ass too, but he much preferred topping, despite pleasure and stimulation back there being good too.

The head of his cock tapered softly, glistening with a drop of pre-cum. A moderate number of chunky, fleshy barbs layered his cock with more around the base, near the tuck of his sheath, his balls hanging fat and heavy below. His fluffy sack would have hidden the light definition between his nuts if they had not been as full as they were, yet he had been holding back in pursuit of the okapi for so long that he ached furiously.

"Unff… You know you're in for it…"

Aydin licked his lips, thrusting down his need as he took control of himself once more, strutting into the showers with all the poise and desire that he held in paw. The tiger's tail swung deviously between him, flicking back and forth, as he stalked his prey, though Eli was already waiting for him.

And the okapi looked simply divine as he stood under the water, his large ears slipped back a little, wiggling faintly, water streaming over his muzzle, darkening the hair across his chest. His cock rose to attention, dark and a little slimmer than Aydin's, though no one could ever have cared about size at a time like that. The rounded tip of his cock pressed into Eli's paw as the okapi smirked seductively and thumbed it, smearing away a drop of pre-cum before the hot water washed it away.

"Why don't you come get me then?" The okapi breathed, lips barely parted, a soft whuffle on his lips. "You've been slavering over me for so long, wanting to claim me, to take me…"

Aydin snarled. With such an open offer laid out before him, the tiger lunged for Eli, seeing only his prey, led by his throbbing dick. His shaft felt as if it was going to burst with desire, yet he had the okapi, *finally*, in his arms, pinning him back to the wall. His tail lashed and he purred throatily as he claimed him, caging Eli in against the wall with his arms while he rolled his hips against the okapi.

"Mmm… Yes, this is what I wanted," he growled, lips breaking into a true smile, relief flooding him at finally having his needs met. "Yes… I need you, little slut. You've been taunting me with that rump of yours. And all I've been thinking about was grabbing you by the tail and dragging you back on my dick so I can fuck that ass of yours…"

Eli quivered and moaned as Aydin's sharp teeth nipped at his throat, playing with him just as the okapi had teased the tiger for so long. Payback had to be given, after all, in due course, but it was the kind of payback both were going to enjoy: exceedingly so.

"Oh… Mmm… Yes, sir…"

The okapi trembled, knees buckling, yet Aydin was right there to pin him with his paw on his shoulder, holding him back firmly to the wall. His paw raked down, careful of his short claws, and he grasped Eli's cock confidently, his fingers wrapping around, stroking up and down a few inches. It was all to test the okapi's readiness, to see whether he really was into it as much as Aydin suspected, yet it was amusing even to him just how wobbly and submissive the okapi became as soon as he was pressed.

He had been so cute teasing him…

"Do you like that, little slut?" Aydin hissed, struggling to keep the smirk off his lips. "Calling me "sir," like you want to be down on your knees for me?

Time to take this dick down your throat, get what you've been damn well gagging for this whole time…"

"Mmm… Yes…"

Eli folded obediently to his knees as Aydin pressed down on his shoulder, though the tiger didn't want to be too rough on him, knowing the floor of the shower area was hard and rough to kneel on for too long. He wouldn't keep the okapi down there for too long, yet he wanted to warm up, to take him and to tease him, to show him exactly what they could play out between one another.

"Suck it…"

Eli whimpered, turning his big, dark eyes up to the tiger. Yet there was only one thing that he could do as the tiger presented his thick, barbed cock to his lips, the tapered, slim tip just right for prying open wanton holes. Aydin growled, rolling his hips forward, spearing his cock into the okapi's mouth as Eli parted his lips for him.

Just for him.

For it did not matter what else the two of them had done or been into, no, not at all, only that they brought to a head every last bit of lust that they had longed for. All that remained were two hot, sweaty bodies, streaming with water, huffing and panting while Aydin fed his thick length down into the back of the okapi's mouth.

"Unff… Yes…" He groaned, blinking through a haze of arousal, relief like nothing he'd felt before washing through him, clean and refreshing. "Fuck, you don't know how long I've been waiting for this…"

The okapi was thieved of the chance to reply by the thick dick in his mouth, forcing his lips wide. As Aydin rested a demanding paw on the back of his head, he curled his fingers around to more firmly, resolutely, hold the okapi in place, relishing in each sensation.

With just the two of them there, he could drag out everything, languishing there, allowing everything to sink into his body.

The heat of the shower streaming over him.

His toes flexing and curling on the hard floor.

How the okapi grunted softly around his girth.

The tentative push into the back of Eli's throat, testing just how much Eli was willing to take.

And the okapi was willing to take it all, every inch of a dick that he craved so terribly. He would not have, after all, teased Aydin so much if he wasn't actually into doing anything for him. Aydin licked his lips and purred as he thrust, rolling his hips to grind into Eli's mouth repeatedly, sliding over his thick, fleshy tongue.

However, Eli had more tricks with his tongue than Aydin had bargained for, winding the long, slippery length all the way around Aydin's cock and dragging it down.

"Oh, fuck, yesssss..."

Letting out a needy hiss, the tiger thrust savagely, grinding, humping. He couldn't even stay still to let Eli do his best work on his dick, thankful only that his barbs were soft enough that Eli did not have to be all that careful not to hurt his own tongue by lapping and suckling. The barbs were even soft enough that they would not, typically, catch and pull uncomfortably at the corners of the okapi's lips, for which Aydin would be exceptionally grateful for later.

Much later. When his brain was fully functioning again, not when he was thrusting into the okapi's sweet muzzle. The wetness slathering his cock was too intoxicating to let anything else take his attention away, not even in the slightest, and Aydin slammed his paw into the shower wall times, growling rudely.

"Ah... Fuck... Yes..."

Aydin growled, flicking his tail, balls feeling tight, even though that was just his mind trying to process the twisting clench of need deep inside him. Fuck, he needed it. He needed it so fucking badly that it felt as if his balls were going to drop off if he didn't get to nut in the hot okapi right there and then. That tongue was divine, dragging and stroking over his cock even as he thrust harder and faster, no finesse or refinement to his thrusts in the slightest. Yet it was more overstimulating than even he could have anticipated, saliva clinging to his dick, so there was always an amount of lubrication between the okapi's tongue and Aydin's cock.

The tiger snarled, licking his lips, the pace of his thrusts picking up more and more. He had wanted to cum in the okapi's rump the first time but – to hell with it! He needed to cum right then, to spend his lusts in the most carnal way possible, grinding his dick all the way up into the back of Eli's throat. Thankfully, the okapi was more than capable of gulping around him to accept the meaty treat as Aydin's barbs raked over his tongue.

"Oh… Yes… Fuck!"

Aydin yowled, curling his toes, his tail lashing – yet it was his cry that betrayed his orgasm to the okapi. He hunched over, rounding above Eli's head, grinding into his muzzle with short, sharp thrusts, as if that was enough to convey his need. Yet it was truly the long, hot spurts of thick tiger spunk shooting straight down Eli's throat that showed the okapi just how desperate he had left the tiger.

True to form, however, Eli gulped everything down he was offered, ignoring the fact his eyes were watering from the strain of taking Aydin's dick into his throat for so long. If Aydin had been in his right mind, he would have pulled back a little to ease the pressure, though it was not as if Eli struggled at all, trying to get away from him. On the contrary, he leaned harder into the pressure with a strangled groan, the soft vibrations from his throat rumbling through Aydin's cock as if he was trying to supply the tiger with a tantalising scrap of additional stimulation.

"Mmmm..."

Aydin breathed heavily, chest heaving, a lazy smile spreading across his lips now that he had had one orgasm. One was not enough, however, but it did clear his mind a little so he could take stock of the situation a little more easily, drawing back as Eli followed his cock. Of course, the okapi did not need to have his mouth free to breathe, breathing through his nostrils, gurgling on the last drops of cum as he strove to swallow them all down without any trouble at all.

Eli blinked and licked his lips, too warm for comfort and yet staying just where he was. There was no need for him to move.

The tiger caught just how he leaned into his paw, cupping his head and playing with his ear. Even though Eli's cock was obviously hard and throbbing, twitching faintly with every pulse of blood through it, the okapi did not make any move to have his needs met. Aydin's brow furrowed, studying him carefully. Perhaps serving and being submissive was what got Eli off?

Ah... No matter. Well, it was a matter – yet Aydin would never be the kind of tiger who didn't take care of his partner. So, the okapi was getting off whether that was what his attention was on or not.

"Come up here," Aydin growled, nudging Eli's thigh with his foot, a softer smile on his face. "Come on now, you can do it."

The gentle encouragement did the trick, even if it was on shaky hooves that the okapi climbed back up on, Aydin taking his weight some so that he did not have to solely support himself. His strong paws gripped the okapi's biceps as he turned him, checking in and ensuring that he was still on board with everything.

"You good?" He purred, his raspy tongue bathing Eli's neck gently as he asked the okapi to face the wall. "Do you need a minute? We got time."

"Ah... No..."

The okapi's voice was wispy and faint, yet grew in strength as his eyes lit up a little more and he glanced back at the tiger, tail flicked to the side. Aydin's eyes could not help but drop to his rump, though they were already pressed quite close together with barely any distance between their bodies. It was a wonderful backside, so thick and round, with a little give to it too, when he rolled his hips and ground against it, sliding his dick between Eli's shivering, fleshy rear cheeks. His cock had not softened in the slightest as he panted and dragged in a deep, raspy breath.

"Yeah... Yeah, I'm fine." Eli groaned, ducking his head between his arms as he braced against the wall, grinding back urgently against Aydin's dick. "I just didn't expect it to be *that* hot... Heh..."

Aydin chuffed a laugh, nipping playfully at the back of Eli's neck. There would be plenty more time for them to get to know one another even more intimately, for the cat had no intention at all of letting all their teasing simply come down to a single fling and only that. No... He liked Eli, what he had seen so far, and was hungry to find out more, presenting his hard-on to the okapi's needy hole as the ungulate relaxed under him.

"Bend your knees a bit, relax..."

The okapi followed his instruction easily, as if it had been what he'd needed and been waiting for all along. To take from his lead alone as Aydin slowly but surely ground into him, stealing Eli's breath away.

"Ah... Ohhhh..."

Eli moaned long and low as his tail hole was taken, sensually spread around a cock that was intent on pleasing him. The tiger rocked his hips, driving in deeply, though even Aydin was surprised at just how easily the okapi opened up around him. It was a sensual heat, truly, closing entirely around his cock from tip to base, spreading his anal ring wide around the girth. Still, he was careful to follow Eli's little cues, the soft grunts that meant he was enjoying it or even if he tensed at any point, needing him to pause and take more time.

Yet it was no time at all before he was thrusting to a pace that suited them both, taking Eli's ass in long, deep strokes, claiming strokes. They were the type of thrusts that, frankly, were intended to leave Eli sore the next morning, overpowering and driving, Eli grunting and groaning as the shower area made their cries bounce in strange and wonderful ways.

The hiss of water over them was nowhere near enough to quell those sounds of lust, however, the tiger's balls bouncing off the okapi's own low hanging pair with every stroke. He would have wondered if he was going too deep for Eli if not for the okapi's hooves scrabbling on the floor and grinding back against him, putting a little rock into his rump just to encourage Aydin on.

"Ah... Please..." Eli moaned, breathless with need. "I'm...so close... Been waiting...so long..."

Ah, so who's the needy one now?

Aydin smirked but, thrusting towards his own orgasm, he wanted to see his submissive of the moment, in all his toned glory, hit his release first. He had already had one climax and part of the pleasure was in the control, in knowing that his cock and attention were both, together, more than enough to bring another into sweet, overpowering bliss. Yet it didn't look like he was going to need to reach around and grasp Eli's cock, more than a little curious if he could get Eli off without using his paws.

He didn't have to wonder for long, angling his hips a little more to grind more closely up over the okapi's prostate, though it was not a very specific grind that time. That would come in time, when he learned exactly what Eli liked, the hot spill of water down his back sending a tingle down his spine.

A few thrusts more was all it took – and then the okapi was chuffing breathlessly, letting loose his seed in long, hot spurts. He must have been rather backed up with cum too, painting the wall with his seed, purely from the raw force of his thrusts. Hissing in his ear, the tiger kept going, not able to stop as he drove himself to that high, that devout peak of need, tail lashing as his glutes clenched.

"Ah… Gonna cum in you…so hard… Ah!"

He yowled, louder than before. It was a good thing that they were alone there in the gym complex, especially as he spent his cream deep inside Eli's backside, rough, heady grinds of his dick keeping his partner spread around him. The tight stretch gripped his cock at Eli's pucker, where the okapi was the tightest, and the tiger's head swam as he climaxed for the second time.

Release was all he needed, time seeming to slow between them, easing to a pace that suited them. The stream of water still marked the passage of time, breath seeming to rasp against his eardrums as Aydin shook his head, tail hanging a little more now that some energy had seeped from his body. Eli was not much better and the tiger purred throatily as he gripped the okapi's hip, holding him steady and firm through their shared lust. Every drop of cum washed away down the shower drain, leaving no evidence behind of their tryst.

Eli shivered and Aydin withdrew just to tuck him under the water a little more, though it was Eli who took the initiative to turn the heat up a little, chuckling breathlessly. His ropey tail swung back against the tiger and Aydin purred, soaking in the moment.

The prey had been *more* than worth the chase.

Things between the tiger and the okapi, jokingly dubbed predator and prey, had not ended. Yet the predator of the duo was still on the hunt.

But what for? The tiger smirked, tail curling as he briefly, though noticeably, touched his muzzle to Eli's cheek.

Oh, he was only hunting to see if he could get Eli's number, of course, to take him out to dinner.

It was the start of something new and someone, undoubtedly, that Aydin had no intention at all of ever letting go of.

Push Ups

Nuka chuckled, the little Arctic fox a good head shorter than the lion, clad in his summer colours. Even though most people thought of Arctic foxes in white fur, when they typically considered them, he had a darker coat in grey-brown, not all the hairs on his body, of course, the same colour. It would have been boring, after all, if everything was uniform, though the tips of his fur appeared brown, particularly when the light shone through them. With the end of summer coming, the fox would soon be back in his white coat to blend in with the snows of winter.

Well, if he wasn't living in a city that was – but anthros were all over the globe by that point. They even worked out to better their physical prowess, not living as their ancestors did and certainly not expending as much energy as had been needed before, in most cases. He was very fortunate, even though he had already finished his workout for the day, to have a lion friend who had a home gym set up in his garage, completely finished with a full cage for heavy lifting, a lifting platform, a full rack of dumbbells, lots of resistance bands, barbells all ready to go – and even a pulley machine.

The main door was closed, for a little more privacy was desired that day with the crisp sense of winter in the air, pulling at their fur as if it yearned to drag them into the darker months of the year already. There was something rugged, however, with how the gym was set up with lighting strips, illuminating all that was needed, while leaving it a little on the rougher side.

Nuka had always liked it, though Cole grumbled about not being able to take progress shots as easily.

The lion huffed under him, nearly to the end of his workout while Nuka was pleasantly sore already, his hide damp with sweat. Neither fox nor lion wore much clothing – just a pair of shorts each and no underwear. Nuka had worked out a while back that Cole didn't usually wear underwear when he had faced a clothing mishap (which was the polite way to put it) while deadlifting. Remembering just how the big cat had got his fuzzy rump exposed still made Nuka laugh.

Not that he would tell the feline that, no. Their relationship was more than comfortable: friends with benefits, sort of. It just didn't feel that casual, as if something more was building, the two of them taking an unconventional route to intimacy. And that was just fine with them as the fox sat cross-legged on top of the lion's back while he completed push up after push up.

"Mmm, you do look good like this…"

The fox teased, rubbing his fingers and the tops of his palms, lightly, along the lion's shoulders, making his tail lash. Cole didn't bother with an answer, however, though he didn't try to do anything to jostle the vulpine off his back anyway. It was an easy way to add some extra weight at the end of a workout with another body, though Nuka was not all that well-placed to hop off if it proved too much for Cole. The fox's attention was too focused on the flex and pull of muscles in the lion's back while he changed his push up to a version with flared elbows, sinking down smoothly all the way to the mats and pushing back up with a grunt.

The fox licked his lips, tasting sweat on the air.

"Come on, Simba, you can do better than that…"

Cole growled.

"You know that's not my name…"

"Well, I'm sure you've called me worse, you know," Nuka quipped back, flicking his thick fox brush behind him. "Concentrate, you still have, like…loads more reps to do."

"I thought you were counting?"

Nuka laughed. He'd make sure Cole got his workout in one way or the other, though it was more alluring than he had any right to admit to watch the lion express his physical prowess. Even more so when he was sitting right there on the feline's lusciously broad back.

"Mmm..."

Nuka couldn't quite help himself, tipping forward to spread his palms out flat on Cole's bare back, digging his fingers in lightly and massaging his rich, brown fur. It was a darker shade by far than what would have been found on a lion out in the wild, but, well, anthros often differed from the species they originated from. With a thick, black mane framing his face, the hair constantly getting in Cole's way, he could never be mistaken, of course, as anything other than a lion.

Yet it was just foreplay, the fox swivelling around and plopping down, with entirely more force than necessary, on the lion's back, his chin resting playfully on the feline's muscular rump. Oh, and what a backside it was, the glutes well-rounded and firm. The lion was going through a cut at that time, limiting his calories, and Nuka was more than happy to adore his body in the meantime, even though he didn't at all mind Cole with a little more weight on him too, when he was bulking up. It was all in the cycle of Cole seeing just how far he could push his body, to see what he could do and just how far he could drive his physical fitness.

"Mmph... Nuka..."

"What?"

The fox grinned, though it was already obvious what he was doing as he hugged the lion's midriff, his chin bobbing with the rise and fall of Cole's buttocks. Those were not his focus, however, not as he slid down the feline's shorts slowly, teasingly, acting as if he wasn't actually going to go that far. Cole always said that he was a "wind up" – or something like that – but Nuka didn't see it. It was all about pushing and stimulating, teasing and bringing a flare of need to the body.

That and the fox really didn't see a better way to ever end a workout other than with Cole's fat cock ramming down his throat. Who wouldn't want a blowjob to get their rocks off when they were cooling down from being all hot and sweaty, muscles trembling with physical fatigue?

It was a good thing, in that case, that the lion and the fox were a good match for each other, Nuka's clever, grasping fingers finding the lion's sheath without even being able to see what he was doing.

"Oh, so you were randy," he teased, running the tip of his finger around the lion's cock, which was slowly protruding from his sheath, just a couple of inches. "You said you didn't want to fuck before working out… Maybe you were the one making me wait, this time, not the other way around."

"Unff…"

Cole was so often a dominant partner and yet there was a certain kind of luxury to be had in putting him in a position where he could not take that top position. Of course, it would not last for long, but Nuka determined to clean every drop of stolen control from it while he could. The fact of the matter was that the lion wouldn't pause his workout, not when he was so close to the end, to take his pleasure, leaving the fox with a little time in which to tease and caress him.

"I can tell you want this," Nuka breathed, rubbing the lion's sheath as his cock more eagerly swelled. "You want to cum in my mouth, holding my head down so I have to take every fucking drop down my throat, hm? I know what you damn well like, Cole… But you're going to do every push up you have left before you get to flex another muscle."

The lion groaned, his voice dangerously silent. That was a bad sign – well, kind of a good sign, as it meant the vulpine was in the good kind of "trouble." Nuka pushed his luck, licking his lips, though the fox ignored the rising state of his own hard-on pressing up needily from his sheath while he ran his questing fingers back over the cat's balls. They were so round and so weighty, so perfectly poised. It was strange to think about the nuts of another male in that way, but someone would have to see Cole in all his naked, muscular glory to contradict that.

And they wouldn't.

So, Cole was all his to enjoy while they tested out the waters of their new, brimming relationship, wherever it was set to go.

All in good time.

He left the lion's balls for the moment, massaging his cock, the palms of his paws running up the smooth length and squeezing softly. Cole didn't have leftover, soft barbs from evolution on his cock, though he did have a lightly defined cone-like head to his cock where the barbs would have been the most numerous (if he had them). The tip was tapered and Nuka smirked as he thumbed it, smearing a dollop of pre-cum across the head and sensitive glands.

"Ngh... Nuka..."

"You got some left, cat," the fox told him, a little imperious in the flick of his ears. "Finish up and then you can do whatever the fuck you want to do with me, Scout's honour."

The feline grumbled, arms trembling as he pressed up again. Nuka shivered, rubbing his fully hard cock up and down, though there was not much variation in his attention that he could give in such a position. He hadn't done it before and he knew that there were other anthros walking by not all that far away, just on the street, No one out there had any damn idea what was going on in the garage, tucked away in an otherwise innocuous residential area.

Nuka liked that thought. But he'd still try to keep his moans under wraps when Cole was fucking his ass later…

Maybe.

The lion shuddered, a reverberation going through his chest as he reached the last reps. One…two…three… Nuka could tell exactly when he was done from how the lion grunted, the pace of the second to last push up increasing slightly, rushing through the motion. Sure, it was awkward in how he rushed to finish but everyone did that, at some point, when they were trying to get through a set of reps.

The next thing he knew was that he was flying through the air. A sense of weightlessness gripped him and Nuka laughed as he was tossed from Cole's back. Whatever level of control he'd stolen from the lion was gone as the randy feline pursued him with a dangerous gleam in his eye.

"Time to put your money…" The lion huffed. "Where your mouth is…"

It was a cheesy line and yet it still managed to send a shudder through the fox, Nuka landing lightly on the matted area and bouncing, rolling to all fours. He just about scrambled up to his knees when the lion was before him, a raging, delicious mass of muscle and fur, his cock jammed right up in the vulpine's face.

"Unff, I see you're – mmph!"

Yet Cole wasn't about to wait for him to catch his breath, seemingly, hooking a finger skilfully into the corner of the fox's mouth and forcing him to open his maw, gaping wide. His cock followed a moment later, sliding in slickly over the fox's flexible, wriggling tongue, driving straight up to the back of his throat.

The lion already knew Nuka could easily take his cock. Especially as Nuka moaned and spread his paws flat on the lion's thighs, greedily drinking in his body in any way he could, the scent of sweat and male musk hanging heavy in the air. It should have been too much for their sensitive noses and yet both lion and fox caught themselves taking great, heady gulps if it, as if they couldn't get enough. It was funny what ended up being good, better than good, in the heat of the moment.

Yet it was right there that Nuka could lose himself. Sure, he had won in making Cole lose control – yet they had both won, in their own way. He was better on the bottom, choking on the lion's prick, and he let Cole have his way with him exactly as he pleased, for he was not about to let the feline go without. He had been the one teasing, after all. Or perhaps the workout itself had been the hot, sweaty, grumbling foreplay they had needed.

Huh… Maybe we both have some odd kinks.

It was not the moment in which Nuka could laugh, however, not as that cock slid over his tongue, forcing it into the gap between his teeth on his lower jaw. He groaned around it but did not push back against the lion at all, merely tightening his grip on the feline's thighs. They were so big, so wide, the muscle taut under his touch, yet the fox yearned for more. His nose crushed softly into Cole's crotch and the thicker ruff of hair there, musky with sweat where it had soaked in throughout their workout, though he would have taken it harder and faster too if he could get more of that scent.

"Mmm…"

He groaned softly, eyelids fluttering closed. There was nothing there that he had to think about, nothing for the fox to worry about in the slightest, only languish there, soaking in the moment. He trembled as the lion thrust rampantly into the back of his throat, speeding up and up, though the fox was used to rougher treatment.

Gentle sex was all good and fun, but he wanted more. He wanted to be fucked hard, fucked roughly, used and taken, again and again. Not thrown away at the end, no, maybe a cuddle... But to have even his sensitive, soft nose grinding into the cat's crotch was everything Nuka craved and more.

He groaned and mumbled around the feline's cock as much as he could, but he was just there to serve him, haplessly trying to flick his tongue up around the head. Just a taste, a little taste... He needed to taste him! And not just the smooth, masculine length of the lion's rod, no, more than that... Yet the fox was hardly in a position where he could take that for himself, which was almost laughable after the position of a trickster that he had gleefully stolen, lying on the lion's back to taunt and tease him.

"Good fox." Cole grunted, as always, a lion of very few words. "Unnghhh... You want to fucking tease... You know you're going to swallow it all."

He moaned his agreement. Yes, yes... That was where he belonged, down on his knees, serving. He would have worshipped Cole's cock and body all day long – and longer still – if he had been allowed to do so, though that would have represented a change in their relationship that they were not, perhaps, quite ready for.

But he could be there in the moment and not think about or worry about anything else. That wasn't for him, no, not in the slightest, not even as the fox drooled around the hot length of meat plugging his muzzle full, letting himself enjoy. It was only with Cole that he had honestly learned how to do that.

And he wasn't turning back again, whimpering and whining, almost embarrassed by how easily he dropped into a deeper state of submission with the lion above him. Yet Cole didn't abuse it, no, not at all, his paw covering the back of the fox's head only to hold him in place as he thrust and thrust, grinding in deep and holding him right where he belonged. There was nothing else for it, even though Nuka's need was set to go unnoticed for just a little longer. He would be taken care of in due course but that moment was about Cole and sucking down his fat prick, letting his tongue caress the underside the best he could.

Not that the fox needed to do much as the lion's throaty, almost strangled, grunts rose, hips speeding up. The fox's ears twitched, catching a muttered curse from the brawny feline, wanting more, aching for it. Every drop, yes... That was what Cole had promised him and it was what he deserved too, he was sure of it. If there was one thing Nuka did well, he was confident in his cock sucking abilities, the slick sheen of his own saliva coating Cole's length.

Closer and closer... The reverberation that ran through the lion's body had Nuka tensing, his tail tucked down, though the fox wasn't trying to cover up or hide any part of his body, oh no. He was content right where he was, scooping his tongue briefly up against the underside of the lion's cock head, right at the moment that the feline roared.

Nuka barely had a moment in which to contain himself as the lion ejaculated, long, hot spurts of thick cum painting the inside of his muzzle. He was forced to swallow quickly in short, needy, desperate gulps, lest he choke on Cole's offering, yet it was something he was more than getting used to. After all, he sucked off the lion after pretty much every gym session they had lately.

And he would never get tired of it: the hot swathes of flesh and muscle, how skin and fur pulled over it, the feral, animalistic scents hanging in the air. He grunted thickly, nose twitching, barely even breathing as he took down all that he could, his jaw aching, a dribble of cum drooling from the corner of his lips where he could not quite take it all the way down. But that was alright. If he knew Cole as well as he thought he did, the lion would have at least one more load for him, perhaps two, before their evening of working out, fucking and hanging out was over and done with.

It was more than he could have hoped for, grinning up at Cole, breathless and panting, as the lion pulled back, something new in the lion's eyes.

Something warmer.

But only the days and weeks and months and more to come would tell just what was to grow between them both…

All from the intoxicating heat of working out together, letting their bodies do exactly what they did best.

Thank you for reading and I hope that these little stories were thoroughly enjoyed, giving you a little break to read and relax!

Are you ready for more? Check out my author website for more furry fiction and where you can purchase my books!

https://linktr.ee/amethystmare

Cover art illustrated by Kai_art; they are contactable via e-mail for work enquiries.

dongvieck10@gmail.com